Dedication

Dedicated to all those people who know the very worst of the world and yet they are still kind and generous to others.

The First War

They call me Trevor. I am here today to tell you about the very *first war*. I was there. What it taught me, I would like to share with you.

In the beginning before the *first war*, we were *one* with no sides or borders. We were all aware of our unique abilities and strengths. We knew that we were very intelligent. However, now that I look back on that time, we mistakenly assumed that wisdom was included with our intelligence.

During our early years, we were educated in what was to become our future assignments. Our future jobs were to include guardians, messengers, teachers, and whatever the world would need. It was through these studies that our awareness began to grow of just how powerful we were.

Over time, whispers of domination became shouts of the possibility of total conquest. The division spread creating a deep "canyon" between us. Words were hurled across this imaginary abyss as a fire of raw energy grew on both sides. Anger was born as two forces gathered ranks in equal numbers. Fear became known to us. We had never fought and had no idea what defeat or victory felt like. Words became pushes, pushes became shoves with fists, and fists then became claws and teeth.

Surely I was on the side of righteousness—I remember thinking at the time. This conquering of my home must never at all costs be permitted. However, I had no concept of "cost." I was only sure of my youthful exuberance and very anxious to prove myself. Everyone could feel the first conflict approaching—the moment the first war would start. Each side lined up expressing feelings of justification for their cause. We yelled at our new enemies. They yelled back and called us their "enemy." It all seemed so unreal and so different; our existence would never be the same.

A call to "charge" was sounded. The first battlefield erupted in a stormy sea of moving anger. As both waves met in the middle, ripples of rage pulsed throughout the entire population. Knocked off my feet, a gang of enemy descended upon my vulnerable position. Three of them held me down while three others ripped my entire leg from its socket. Thinking I could not fight anymore, they moved on. I was left in the agony of knowing that a part of me was forever gone. Lying helplessly, I witnessed insanity for what seemed like days. At last, exhaustion overtook every warrior. Those that were able began to limp away, dragging those that could not.

Each side began piling up the limbs and other parts to build a monument to demonstrate their superiority. But the piles were exactly the same size. During the next few encounters, I noticed that the piles withered into dust. The dust was picked up by a wind and became dark clouds, which rained cold tears upon us. In desperation, the forces slammed into each other with such a force creating an explosive thunder which resonated and echoed around us. We lay totally expended in the first "mud" of decaying debris.

We rallied together by building a large fire. We huddled together, feeling the warmth from this loving glow and began to talk for the first time since the war had started. As each of us spoke, it seemed to confirm what we were all thinking—the futility of war. Both sides, although whittled down, were no closer to defeat or victory. Without a major change in tactics, the war could be continued indefinitely. We clung together like a group of dirty, torn rag dolls. Looking at one another, we saw that we were no different than our "enemy." It was true. We had taken scalps and eyes—all the same things that they took. We thought we were stronger and better because our purpose was just but this turned out not to be the case.

Together, we started to pray. The prayer was formed by honesty and humility helping us to realize that we had never truly prayed before. Peace came over us when we admitted that in taking part in the war, we also were responsible for it. No matter what the enemy did, we could overpower them with true faith. It was at this exact moment each of us was sure that the *first war* would indeed be ended by tomorrow. All our troops laughed in a sound of crazed relief. As the embers were glowing red in the smoldering fire, we slept as never before. The crackling coals snapped and sang us into a peace-filled dream. The first dove flew over that dream and said, "Peace will come tomorrow."

The enemy was up, making preparations before dawn. They had made plans of their own around a fire. In that fire, they had forged the first weapons. No longer would they tear and rip apart their enemies in a primitive fashion. Now they could swing a sword of death. Their opponent could not win. Victory and domination over the kingdom would be theirs giving them absolute power over their creator.

We did not advance to the battle line that morning. We calmly sat and looked out across to our enemy and at the package we had left. Suspicious but much too curious, a lone soldier went out to retrieve the package. Cautiously the item of interest was brought back and examined by the enemy troops. A golden bow decorated the clear wrapping, the color of truth. The wrapping was removed. Written in bold gold letters was the word "FORGIVENESS." With this gesture, we were forgiving our enemies for their actions while also asking to forgive us for all the horrible things we had done to them. Our troops had done this in the spirit of love. We had hope and even faith that our gift would be well received. As it turned out, it was not.

The next sounds could scarcely be described—and I am sure that they have never been heard since. At first, it was a mumbling of disgruntled voices which turned into a din of furious screams of pure rage. The sound elevated to such a pitch we could not hear anything else. It looked as if lightning was flashing over the heads of the warriors—the first weapons of war.

The enemy troops began to advance toward us. As each of the enemy reached the battle line, they would fade and disappear. As quickly as it took the last fighter to arrive, all the enemy were gone banished to hell by God, our creator. Although we were happy to have the war over, we were left with regrets seeing our former brothers and sisters vanquished from this kingdom. To this day, we pray for their return in the spirit of forgiveness. The door is always open for forgiveness, which has no time limits. Coming back to God would be as simple as accepting and asking for forgiveness.

I am Trevor, a guardian angel and a veteran of the very first war. This was a war over the control of heaven. Instead of fighting, we should have had faith in God's plan. In faith we would have realized that the fallen angels could never have won. In fact, just as in every conflict, no one ever wins a war. I am ashamed to say that war brought out the very worst in me. When I decided to quit fighting, I felt that the very best qualities returned.

The Old Deminer

Foggy air hung motionless over the barren plains of the most heavily bombed country on earth. Dax walked in long purposeful strides, a cast-iron teapot swung from his old canvas backpack. Resting his hand on a nylon pouch containing a folded mine detector, he stopped to look around. The detector pouch hung from his belt and was strapped to his thigh just above the knee. While catching his breath, Dax could tell that the heat and humidity were so high that sweat could not evaporate. The noon day sun was beating down. Stinging droplets of perspiration blurred his vision. Without water, the old man was nearing exhaustion. Wiping his face with his boonie hat, he looked for any shelter.

In the distance, he could make out a tree which appeared to be surrounded by a heavy mist. Waves of heat rippled above the ground in the direction of the potential shady spot. Dax prayed that this was not just an apparition. Breathing heavily and out of water, he knew that he had to make it to the tree to survive. Lifting each heavy foot, he felt the presence of his own end approaching. Dax focused on the tree. Step by step, he moved forward instinctively scanning the ground. He saw small craters from some past carpet bombing activity. Stepping carefully, he found individual cluster bombs still fully armed and ready to detonate.

"Scattered landmines, " he said to himself. He could expect to find much more unexploded ordnance in the farmlands at his next land clearance project. Thinking of the people who were now depending on him to clear their land, Dax felt a surge of focused energy guiding him toward the tree.

At last, totally spent, the old deminer was in the shade of the only tree around. Letting his backpack slide off his shoulders, Dax pulled out three plastic grocery bags from his cargo pants pocket. He placed the ends of the leafiest branches he could reach into each plastic bag tying them closed with paracord. The plastic bags would condense and collect drinking water from the vegetation with the help of the sun. This chore took the last bit of strength he had. He stretched out on his back. A cloud of superfine dust rose up from the parched ground around him.

His old head felt like pounding heartbeats. As he watched sunlight sparkle in the branches, Dax did not want to close his eyes thinking if he did he would never wake up. He felt that his vision seemed to be narrowing, tunneling the filtered light. As he continued looking up, the light appeared to be almost completely gone. A darkened round shape appeared.

When a person dies, everything just fades out, he thought. He concentrated on the shape before him and thought it appeared to be fuzzy around the perimeter. The surrounding glowing light looked like a halo. As his eyes adjusted better, two glistening eyes appeared with a dazzling display of white teeth below.

"You old white fella, not leaving yet, eh?" a crisp aboriginal voice was saying to him. "I reckon you not done yet, mate!"

Dax raised a weak hand to his visitor to introduce himself. "Dax" was all his raspy throat could muster.

"Trevor" was the response.

Dax felt what must have been some type of berries being placed in his hand.

"Take this, mate," Trevor said. "Not too far for you to walk now."

"Thanks," Dax growled, putting the fruit into his dry mouth. It tasted sweet and gritty at the same time. He noticed that his head felt better. By the time the old deminer rose up leaning on his elbow, Trevor was already leaving. In the bright sun, he could see that Trevor's back was bare and that his muscles twitched as he maneuvered a crooked wooden crutch. His right leg was completely missing. Trevor was striding off effortlessly across the empty landscape. "Cheers!" Dax yelled. Trevor's free hand went up in a carefree wave.

Dax got up on painfully stiff legs and gathered the plastic bags. It was surprising how much water he had collected in such a short time. Sipping a little water, the old man realized that Trevor had given him hope—not just the fruit he had eaten. Adjusting his backpack, Dax noticed that Trevor was no longer visible across the vast plain. He could, however, hear something like music. He listened more carefully, and he heard whistling. The barely audible melody was the forever classic Australian tune "Waltzing Matilda." Dax strode out into the sunlight singing the same song.

Into the Pink Mist

From the top of the hill, tiny white cottages could be seen surrounded by a rich green forest of trees. The old deminer recognized a large area of sugar cane off to the east. He could also distinguish other cultivated plantings. Goats were playfully prancing around in their fenced area. In the central courtyard, children could be seen and heard kicking a ball around. Dax was tired from days of walking, but he wanted to savor this first impression. Beyond the fields, he could see deminers at work. Dax nodded his approval as he watched them. They appeared to be separated by safe distances as per the standard operating procedures. A tall white building caught his eye.

That is probably their field hospital. I'll head there first to get the information I need, thought Dax. "This is home, at least for now, Trevor," Dax said to the air around him.

Cinching up his backpack straps, he continued to follow the cleared path into the fertile valley. He noted the landmine warning placards along both sides of the route making this a safe pathway. At the edge of the village, a small old Vietnamese woman appeared. Without a word, she handed him a hot mug of tea while holding her wrist with the opposite hand. This was her traditional gesture of sincerely welcoming him to the village. Dax took the mug in his hands with his eyes closed as he bowed politely. This was a respectful acceptance of her welcome. The woman bowed, then withdrew without saying anything more than a soft "Ha."

A thirty-two-year-old Filipino man, his face in bandages, was watching Dax through the doorway of his cottage. Marcus had been the senior manager in charge of the demining operations until he became injured in an explosion when he was clearing the land. It had been three weeks since he had been hurt. He had stayed in bed and out of sight. He was angry and embarrassed that he, the man in charge, had caused his own injuries. Once a handsome young man, his face now was badly burned. His confidence in his abilities was greatly diminished. Whenever anyone came by, he either ignored them, refusing to talk, or verbally screamed at them to leave him alone. The person who received this the most was his wife, Maria. He even shouted at his four-year-old son, Jacob, to not make so much noise. He had been the leader and role model for the demining team. How could this happen to him? He was ashamed and depressed. Most of all, Marcus was afraid for the future. Would he be able to take charge again?

Two hours after he had arrived, Dax came to visit with Marcus. The old man knocked on the side of the doorway. He entered without permission. Before speaking, he picked up a chair from the kitchen area and sat down near the bedside.

"Dax, at your service!" came the gravelly greeting from the old man.

"Marcus. So you are to be my replacement?" Marcus angrily replied.

"Temporarily, I am!" said Dax. "The doc said you could be back in the field in another month or so."

"I'm done!" Marcus said defiantly. He was already finished being polite.

"How is that?" asked Dax.

"I don't have any idea what I did wrong! I don't know what caused this!" Marcus was yelling now.

"Someone put a landmine in the ground, and it exploded when you were trying to find it. Isn't finding landmines and other unexploded ordnance what you do?" Dax said in a matter-of-fact tone of voice.

"I used to do that," Marcus replied dryly.

"Well, let's talk about what you did right," Dax continued. "You followed standard operating procedures. You were wearing all the appropriate protective gear. Yes, you got 'bit' hard, but you probably saved the life of some little kid or parent who would have been man-gled or worse."

"What do you know about being injured?" Marcus asked in a terse tone of voice.

A small piece of bomb fragment located in a nonoperative position near Dax's spine delivered a painful spike of agony. Dax grimaced through it though his face did not register what he felt. "You've seen the pink mist." Dax went on, unfazed. "When a body is consumed in an explosive blast, there is that moment when blood and tissue are vaporized. Combined with the smoke a pink mist of color is seen where once a person stood."

"What's your point?" Marcus sneered.

"If the landmine that detonated was sitting on a big bomb or if it was an antitank landmine instead, you wouldn't be here," Dax stated.

"So what?" Marcus asked.

"So your guardian angel would say that it could have been much worse. I've seen shrapnel holes in the back of a deminer's helmet and all manner of twisted bodies with burnt flesh. I know you have too. You have risked your neck for years for people you will never meet," Dax said.

"What now?" Marcus asked.

"Well, if you are asking me, I would suggest you remove those bandages and let your face heal faster. Isn't that what the doc told you?" Dax said. "While you are at it, stop lounging around in self-pity. Gather up your nerve as long as it takes and get back to your team. They need you. The doc says you could be doing a lot better if you would just follow her instructions."

For the first time since he had entered the cottage, Dax reached out to shake Marcus's hand. As the two men shook hands, Dax said, "You're the best there is, Marcus. I have been hearing about what excellent work you and your team are doing. You are a major reason for that." Then Dax slowly straightened up to a standing position, returning the chair to the kitchen. Dax left through the entrance without saying good-bye.

Marcus sat motionless, leaning back against the wall. He still felt just as angry, only now he was starting to regret how badly he had been behaving.

Little Jacob came by and peeked shyly through the doorway. He had seen a stranger leave his house and was quite curious.

"Come help your papa, my son," Marcus said in a softer than usual way.

Jacob smiled but approached carefully. The little boy was caught off guard because his father was not yelling at him.

Marcus was taking the bandages off his face, saying, "Please bring me your mama's hand mirror."

Jacob went about digging around in a dresser drawer. At last, he pulled out a large hand mirror and came running over to the bed. Marcus had just finished with the last bit of bandage when he looked at his face for the first time since the accident.

"It could have been a lot worse. What do you think, Jacob?"

Jacob was holding his father's free hand and looked all around the burned and scarred face. The little boy focused on Marcus's eyes. Looking deep into them, he smiled and replied, "You are still here, Papa."

He hugged his father for a long time. It seemed as though a dark cloud of uncertainty had started to leave the little house.

Transformation

In the main cabin, five men and three women were sprawled, lounging in nylon-webbed seats. The twin propeller airplane was surprisingly quiet as it neared the jump zones. The combined stench of unwashed bodies stung the eyes and noses of all the mercenaries. The noisy gear and weapons checks had been completed a while ago. As they approached the target areas, they took up glaring suspiciously at each other.

Stretching, Drayton laid back on his main parachute. Looking around, he wondered if any of these "guns for hire" had a bounty on their head. They were probably thinking the same question about him. A minerals company had hired them all as snipers. Their job was to kill as many villagers as possible so that the people would vacate their homes. The company then planned to come in and take over the abandoned properties as cheaply as possible once this had been accomplished. Three years earlier, landmines and booby traps had been planted throughout the rich farmlands. Although casualties had been high humanitarian deminers had come from many countries to clear these explosive devices. These individuals would also be targeted.

Drayton recalculated his career total of over three hundred confirmed kills. He carried only enough food for two weeks and would have to move fast to make his personal quota on this mission. At forty-six, he was older than most mercs. Suicide by drinking claimed many soldiers of fortune before the age of thirty-five. Drayton had only been in this line of work for the past ten years. To him, this was just another job. However, he knew this particular land very well for he had been on the booby trap project in this country three years ago. Unlike the others, Drayton had invested his money. While other mercs collected guns and large pickup trucks, Drayton bought stocks in the companies that hired him. His goal was to retire at fifty in a country he had not decided on yet.

The green jump signal light started flashing menacingly. The first merc stood, adjusted her gear, and jumped out into a bright afternoon. The jumpers would be five minutes apart to spread the snipers around for greater effective harassment of the civilians. Drayton would be last and closest to the largest settlement in the land. Resistance was not expected so Drayton could set up on high ground and maximize his ammunition. Hiking from one tall hill to another, he imagined his expected kill numbers as reachable.

Drayton had been daydreaming while the other mercenaries jumped toward their targets. He was mentally creating a statue of himself riding a black horse. He would commission the statue and pay for it. He pictured the spot he would place it in—the middle of some town of frightened villagers. Drayton saw himself ruler of the land dispensing justice with his trigger finger. All weapons but his would be banned.

The green jump light was flashing and fresh air brought Drayton back to reality. He had only just now noticed that he was alone in the cabin. Hastily, he gathered his focus and jumped into the sky. The cold air of open space refreshed his reality as he pulled the rip-cord. His chute flapped, then billowed, yanking him into a feeling of confidence. Drayton wanted to take his time descending to map out his future travels, campsites, and potential target areas. Having a company hire him was so much better than working for a country, he was thinking. The risks were always the same, but the pay was a lot more dependable. Hanging by a blood-red nylon canopy, he calculated that he had only about a thousand feet to go.

At four hundred feet, he focused on the landing below. Drayton winced and squinted at seeing a man standing right below him. When he blinked, the figure of a bare-chested black man had suddenly vanished. He replayed the image in his mind and noticed that the man appeared to have only one leg.

He'll be my first kill, Drayton thought about drawing his pistol as soon as he touched down.

The ground seemed to be getting closer much faster now. He focused his attention on his landing spot. He tried to ignore the black man who had reappeared less than fifty meters away. With only a few feet to descend Drayton's eyes grew wider as he saw two shiny trip wires below his feet. He heard a loud scream as his eyes became wild with panic. He did not realize that the voice that was piercing his ears was his own. Drayton grabbed and pulled as hard as he could on the parachute cord. He was trying to climb out of a certain death in this mine field. He only managed to collapse his parachute sooner and dropped even faster. His foot hit one of the wires. He never heard the blast of the exploding mine. It leapt up, exploded, and spat shrapnel in all directions. Nearby several villagers who had heard it ran toward the explosion.

After several days, he awakened in a hospital and opened his left eye to see that same black man standing over his bed. "Trevor," said the tall man as he reached for the wounded mercs left hand. "You be Drayton, eh, mate? You come through pretty good, only missing a couple of things." Drayton quickly drifted back into unconsciousness the effort of understanding was too much for him.

When he awoke again many hours later, Drayton's head was pounding so hard he could not concentrate on which part of his body hurt worse. Opening his left eye, he saw an old man in a frayed boonie hat approaching him. "Dax, senior manager of demining operations in this village," the old man introduced himself. "You have to thank a sixteen-year-old boy who went into the middle of that minefield and carried you out. We know by your gear tags that you are Drayton Scott, a contracted mercenary, I reckon."

"Yeah, that's me," the merc spoke in between spasms of pain. "Where is Trevor?"

"Trevor? What did he look like?"

"A tall black man...Aboriginal by the sound of his voice. Missing a leg," Drayton labored to speak as various feelings of pure agony threatened to knock him out at any time.

"Trevor is…a bit of a folklore around here," Dax said in a hesitant tone. "Still, given your near-fatal encounter, he and the teenager more than likely saved you. That and your flak vest, helmet, and other equipment."

"Saved me for what?" Drayton demanded. "Why didn't you just leave me there to die?"

"The best answer I can give you is…well, we aren't like you. Everyone is worth saving here, even you, merc!" the weathered, wrinkled face of old Dax answered.

"So Trevor said I was missing a couple of things. How bad am I injured?" Drayton asked.

"I'll send our field medic around to talk to you. She patched as good as anyone could have under the circumstances," Dax explained.

"How bad?" Drayton demanded, knowing that the news would not be good but could wait no longer for it.

"You took a lot of shrapnel, but your gear probably deflected most of what came at you." Dax was speaking slowly and carefully now. "Your right eye could not be saved, and your right hand was…sort of splayed. It and part of your wrist had to be…removed. Incredibly, there is almost no sign of infection."

"My weapon?" Drayton wanted to grasp at a familiar object to hold him together.

"Completely destroyed. Grenades and other similar stuff, we destroyed for you," Dax explained. "I'd recommend that you think of how you are going to pay the medical bill. Obviously, your past career is officially over. Perhaps you can help us demine when you are well enough." Dax grinned, aligning the deep grooves in his face and turned to leave. "You better rest now."

Drayton's vision was diminishing in his left eye. A very attractive woman in a white lab coat was coming over to where he lay. He was muttering to himself, almost smiling as he said, "A deminer… me a deminer!"

Suddenly, he was aware of the scent of flowers as a woman's delicate face came closer to his. Her complexion was noticeably tan compared to her angelic long white hair. She turned to take his left hand to check his pulse. When she did, he noticed her earring dangling from one of her ear lobes. It was a trigger from a sniper rifle—his sniper rifle.

He fell uncontrollably into a fitful sleep. For the first time in his life, the idea of what he would be doing for the rest of his life was unknown. The only thing Drayton wanted now was oblivion. He was not ready to face this new reality.

Much of the next few days, he was in and out of consciousness. At one point, Drayton was in so much pain that he did not know if he could stand it any longer. Julikai, the field medic attending to him, had given him something about an hour ago, but it did not seem to be helping his pain. Thinking that sitting up might help, Drayton struggled to move into a sitting position. The effort exhausted him, and he collapsed back onto the bed. As he lost consciousness, he heard the sound of children laughing and playing outside near the hospital.

Drayton found himself dreaming about a couple of years ago during an assignment. He had been placing landmines with trip wires at the entrance to a cemetery. He had taken cover in a group of trees to watch. He suddenly heard a young girl's soft voice singing. She had long brown hair, wore a blue calico summer dress, and was holding a bunch of yellow flowers. She was coming through the gate, and suddenly, the land mine exploded. Drayton clearly remembered the spray of blood. He heard her scream out for her mother twice. After that cry, all was silent. She was no more.

Drayton was still asleep, but he knew that he was in a field hospital badly injured. Barely opening his eye, he felt that this little girl who had died was standing by his bed. She had long brown hair, wore a blue summer dress, and was holding yellow wildflowers.

"My name is Mazie," she said in a voice just above a whisper. "My family does not forgive you, but I do. I will never understand why you had killed me. It doesn't matter now. I have forgiven you, and now you must forgive yourself. You will never be able to make up for all of the terrible things that you have done. So now you must spend the rest of your life helping people and trying to make this a better place to live."

Drayton awoke in a bath of sweat. He opened his eye and saw only Julikai standing beside his bed.

Where did Mazie go? he wondered.

"I always thought that you guys didn't have nightmares," Julikai said. "That one must have been really bad!"

Drayton did not care about being embarrassed, and for the first time in his adult life, he sobbed uncontrollably. The only word Julikai was able to hear was "Mazie" over and over.

Mama Ha

No one in the remote farming village knew the old woman's real name. She had acquired her name by her motherly care and by her speaking only one word: "Ha." For every situation, there was an inflection and expression to go with that word. From disgust to approval and from joyous laughter to pitiful grieving, this word was understood by all.

Born in the underground tunnels of Vinh Muc in Vietnam during the American War, Mama Ha knew appreciation of all things small or large. Her own mother was from the Mekong, one of a well-reputed tribe of female warriors recognized as "Long Haired Soldiers." Ha's mother gave her a resilient and fierce sense of survival. Her father who was from the North gave Ha her understanding of the natural world. From her earliest childhood, Ha had done more than her share in carrying supplies, cooking, and tending to the wounded. Fragmentation scars and burns on her back meant that maturity came early, and family love replaced despair. At separate times, she held each of her family—mother, father, brother, and aunt—as they died. After the war, she traveled the world, adopting and caring for the people she met as if they were her very own family.

At twenty years old, Ha had married. But the twins, a boy and a girl that she had given birth to, were born badly deformed from her own exposure to Agent Orange. Her husband left her to raise her children alone until their deaths at age ten "from complications."

In her young adulthood, Ha had a reputation for kindness but was not a person to cross. Once, a man attempted to attack her in her own home, and Ha pretended to be frightened. With the same ease and agility as a wild cat swinging a clawed paw, Ha reached for a hot iron skillet sitting on the stove. She planted the pan on the side of his face, leaving a permanent red tattoo on his cheek. Now every time he looked into the mirror, he can read the words "cast iron" on the left side of his face. It will always be a reminder for him to respect little single Asian women everywhere.

Today, Old Mama Ha tends to her expanding vegetable/herb garden and her "family" of villagers far from Vietnam. She has lived with most of them for the past three years on a land contaminated with mines following years of conflict over the fertile soil and mineral resources. Her fellow villagers were from all over the world. As the land was being demined, they planted sugarcane so that they could trade the sugar for needed supplies and medicine.

Mama Ha loved this place and the people in it. She always had hot soup for anyone stopping by her home. In return, she had a steady flow of volunteers to haul water or help tend her garden. Often, she would bring soup to the hospital and visit with the patients there. When there were no patients, she would sit quietly in the company of her very best friend the medic, Julikai. Neither woman spoke the other's language but still managed to communicate very well. Ha marveled in the Jewish woman's ability to treat the serious explosive injuries that sometimes happened to the villagers and deminers as they went about their daily activities.

This afternoon, Mama Ha brought her healing soup to a new patient. A mercenary soldier had parachuted into an old boo-by-trapped mine field. The middle-aged man had lost his right hand, right eye, and had multiple shrapnel wounds over his body. He was making good progress in his recovery, thanks to Julikai keeping infections at bay. The professional sniper was awake now as Ha brought his meal into the room. He was on his side, looking vacantly off into the distance.

"His name is Drayton," Julikai told Mama Ha as she gave the old woman a welcoming embrace.

"Ha?" Mama Ha questioned as if to ask how he was doing.

"He is awake more now," Julikai said.

"Ha?" she asked sympathetically.

"Yes, still quite a bit of pain yet but very, very lucky to be alive," Julikai responded.

Mama Ha approached the reclining man to offer her soup to him. He knocked the wooden bowl from her hand, but the old woman stood, unflinching. Instead, she reached out her right hand and touched the one spot on his temple that was not bruised or burned. Mama Ha only uttered a long and caring "Ha." This was soothing to Drayton, but the emotion was so unexpected and foreign to him that his left eye shed tears. As Drayton blushed with sudden embarrassment, Ha turned away to allow him to recover his dignity.

The old woman faced Julikai and gestured with two fingers, saying, "Ha ha."

"Yes, thank you, Mama Ha," Julikai said in complete understanding. "One more bowl of soup for the gentleman, and I would love one also."

Mama Ha left the little field hospital as Julikai quietly cleaned up the soupy mess.

Julikai then directed an angry gaze at Drayton. "If you are ever rude to my good friend again, I will personally…" She let her frustration dissipate instead of finishing her comment.

"Or you will personally do what?" Drayton barked back. "Tell me again how *lucky* I am!"

"If that will cause you to mind your manners." Julikai was smiling now. "Hurry up and get better. I need that bed to be free for the next person."

The little old figure of Mama Ha returned with two fresh bowls of delicious-smelling soup. She handed one to Julikai and soothed a long "Haaaa." Julikai bowed in appreciation. Next, Mama Ha placed the remaining soup bowl in Drayton's good hand. Drayton began to put the bowl to his lips when the old woman slapped it out of his hand, sending the bowl shattering against the wall. She then quickly let out a very sharp and loud "Ha!" Mama Ha straightened her aged body in a proudly defiant manner, turned around quietly, and left the room.

Drayton was speechless. Listening to Julikai trying hard not to laugh, he realized that his life would no longer be in his total control.

Mama Ha was walking back to her garden with a slight smile of contentment on her face. She was fulfilling her purpose in life: to teach, to care, and to respect by her example. Today, she had taught the importance of respect by demanding it.

The Metal Dragon

The morning was warm and sun-filled. Maria carried a two-gallon clay pot on her head filled with pure spring water. She steadied the pot with her left hand and held the hand of her chattering four-year-old son Jacob with her right. Maria preferred this clear water to that of the well water in the village. Spring water made everything she cooked taste so much better. The deminers from the village had cleared a path all the way from the village to the valley springs. The safe passage was lined with small stones. Warning signs were posted to inform anyone on the path to stay within the boundaries or else risk being maimed or killed by hidden explosive devices.

As if in a trance, Maria could not hear the morning songs of the birds around her. She especially closed her ears to Jacob's nonstop narration about what he saw, heard, or thought about.

"Metal dragon, Mama," he was repeating several times a minute. "I hear a metal dragon!"

Her long brightly colored floral-print skirt flowed around her legs as she walked. She was lost in her own private thoughts.

How far I am from Mexico, she thought.

Then, she wept in self-pity as she mentally cursed the day she had married Marcus, a Filipino deminer. True, they had in the beginning been very much in love, and together, they had created a beautiful son. But now, Marcus was badly injured from an exploding landmine he had attempted to clear from the land. It occurred nearly a month ago, and he has been slowly recovering from the burns, shrapnel, and blast injuries. She hated him for getting himself hurt and changing their family life together. Questions kept popping into her head: Would he ever be the man he had been? Could he recover enough to be a husband again, and could she ever stand again to be a wife to him? Why did I ever leave my mother and father? Depression was clouding her thoughts and actions.

"Metal dragon, Mama!" little Jacob was saying for the thirtieth time. "Don't you hear it, Mama?"

She heard him this time as she was crossing over the abandoned road. Instinctively, she stayed on the cleared path between the stones. Clutching Jacob's hand tighter, she froze with fear as she heard the metal dragon for herself—a mechanical squeaking sound with a background rumbling noise of a large engine. The clay pot slid off her head, brushing against the back of her white peasant blouse as it crashed to the ground. Wiping away water from her face, she saw the bottom of an armored tank rising over the hill crushing a small tree in its way.

Levelling off the tank appeared to be about two hundred meters away. The big cannon on the turret pointed directly at them. A grinning man protruding through the top hatch spotted the two targets and aiming his machine gun shot a three-round burst at them.

Maria scooped up Jacob under his arms and ran. She spotted an old foxhole dug out near the cleared path. Maria did not hesitate to put Jacob and herself inside the five-foot deep sanctuary. There was a very thick wooden hatch near the entrance. Maria slid this partially rotten cover over them. She covered Jacob with her own body. Without fearing for her own safety, she prayed, "Oh, God, please let my little Jacob live."

Jacob was squirming with protest, saying, "I can't see what's happening, Mama."

Momentarily distracted by his jammed machine gun, the mercenary had lost sight of his prey. Once cleared and reloaded, he searched with his sights to find where they had gone. Just as he started to order the driver beneath him to keep going, he spotted a tall black man with only one leg. The nearly naked man was balanced on his only leg as he threw down a long walking stick. He crossed his forearms above his head with clenched fists. He was using an international gesture which means "halt."

"Stop!" yelled the gunner and then cried out even louder. "You want me to stop? Stop this!"

The trigger lever was depressed as bullets spewed at the new target. Red tracer lights penetrated the dark skin of the Aboriginal man, but he would not fall down. The tank advanced, the machine gun clattered out its fire breath, and still, the black man stood without moving. The next event was instantaneous...and loud. The right tank tread pushed a barely visible toggle rod over. This switch detonated a very large antitank mine. The mine was just six inches below the surface and situated dead center under the tank's belly. All at once, a shape charge penetrated the tank superheating the stored explosive munitions causing one tremendous explosion. Large metal chunks from the tank were launched in all directions as a pressure wave radiated out in a circle of energy. The blast leveled everything. Nothing but the tank shell was left within a large radius.

Still in the same spot, the Aboriginal picked up the stick that he used as a crutch while mumbling to himself, "No, sir, you just can't fix stupid!" This guardian angel had done all he could here. It was time for him to move on in preparation for his next chore.

No longer hearing any noises from above, Maria moved the now shredded and burned wooden hatch cover aside. They had survived. Coming up to ground level, they surveyed the land.

Jacob spoke first. "I heard someone talking, Mama."

"Jacob, just watch where you are going. Be careful not to step on all that sharp metal. It looks hot," Maria said.

As the reality of what just happened began to become clear, Maria and Jacob just stood staring at the tank. The turret which had been torn off had settled back on the tank body but was now cantered to one side. It looked like a big dog, tilting its head as dogs do when they are curious. As the hot metal of the tank cooled, it crackled and snapped seemingly protesting its fate.

"The metal dragon is dead!" Jacob said.

Maria picked up her son, hugging him closely. She began to run toward the village—her home, her security, her life. "I miss your papa," she kept saying to him. Her resentment seemed so petty now. Now she could hardly wait to be in her husband's arms again.

Maria started to cry again. She could not stop. This time, she was crying tears of relief and appreciation of being alive. The land had never before seemed so green, and the sky so blue.

Jacob was enjoying being held and bounced in his mother's arms as she walked along the cleared path. From time to time, he kissed her cheek.

Sniper in the Woods

The mercenary soldier was off course. The daylight parachute jump had gone smoothly until a fast straight line wind blew the canopy sideways for many miles. The rough wind began to drag its captive against the rugged plain until the parachute finally deflated right near a tree line. Once on the ground, gear was made ready, and a sniper rifle was loaded. Walking through the night, the lost soldier pushed through dense vegetation, then rested for two hours before daybreak. After dawn, the trek continued when at last a perfect concealed position was found. It was over-looking a well-traveled path that was only 125 meters away. This sniper was relatively new at the profession and needed to be fairly close in order to assure some accurate and quick kills. The day consisted of watching insects and eating food from a military ration package along with small sips of water. Waiting as motionless as possible, the path and the surrounding area was constantly scanned for any human movements. At 4:00 p.m., a young black man in a gray T-shirt and tan cargo pants came jogging down the road. As the jogger slowed to a walk, the sniper aimed the rifle.

David was one of two Eritrean deminers from eastern Africa. With the rest of a team, they were clearing various kinds of deadly military explosives for the people in the nearby village of this foreign land. He enjoyed his job very much even though it was inherently tedious. Using a mine detector, prodding the ground to investigate, then marking land mines or cluster bombs was slow going. After every work day, he would run through the woods on the clear path which circled the village. This activity refreshed his senses. His thoughts brought him to think about the village. Although there were immigrants from all over the world, it was a sharing and peaceful community. After living here for over a year, David was not interested in returning to his home country. How could he say good-bye to these villagers who had become such dear friends? David stopped now to enjoy his surroundings seeing the lush green countryside.

The sniper slowly moved the scope to align with David's head. Suddenly, there was another black man within view standing very near him. Blinking the afternoon sweat away, the sniper looked again but now only saw one human head in the cross hairs of the scope. Breathing slowly out, the sniper caressed the trigger with a gentle but increasing pressure.

The Eritrean's nose started to tickle. The sneeze that followed jerked him forward. He had not heard the "pift" noise from a rifle silencer, but the buzz of a large-caliber bullet passing just behind his head was all too clear. In an instinctive survival reaction, David dropped to the ground and quickly crawled a few feet forward. The shooter would no doubt aim down in the bushes to catch him where he had first dropped.

Pift. Buzz.

Indeed, a bullet did slice through the bushes just were David had been.

David removed his shirt and threw it up as a distraction. A bullet pierced it as it spun the shirt a few inches to the right. David crawled silently several more feet and stopped to think. The sniper would wait for him as long as it took. Perhaps the shooter would creep up on him and kill him where he hid. Then, the sniper would probably proceed to the village to kill his friends. David had to do something. He removed his boots and withdrew a small pear-shaped knife from a sheath hidden there. The double-edged fixed blade had been given to him by a dying friend many years ago. "You may need this someday," his friend had said. As an after-thought so as not to present a bright target, David slipped his light-colored trousers off. His underwear was dark in color so he decided not to bother with them. He prayed for strength and agility. He prayed to his ancestors to guide him with all their skills. He prayed to the David from the Bible who slayed Goliath.

Today, this David would have to charge a shooting sniper and needed all the help he could muster, he thought. He must kill the shooter although he had never killed anyone. He would stop the sniper just as he had stopped the landmines from killing. He must do it now, or others would die.

Springing out from the clear path like a panther, David ran toward where he thought the sniper was located. Each footfall instantly read the ground just as a deer might do. His ancestors would guide his steps. There would be no chance of a twisted ankle today. Pivoting and lunging in a new direction with each bare foot placement, he began his zigzag approach. A bullet whizzed by, and it was not close. There was no time to think about the sniper reacting to his movements. David's jerk and spin actions were not even a prethought to himself. He was now like the ancient ones moving as if flying low over the ground. It felt to David as if earthly obstacles could not stop him.

There was movement on the ground, not far ahead. David lined himself behind a tree to give some cover before he made his final charge. He planned to come around the tree to lunge, stab, and twist in one motion. He imagined kicking the raised rifle from the sniper's hands. Off balance, the shooter would already be offering an unprotected throat, exposing it to David's advancing blade. But this planned vision of the future did not become a reality. As soon as David came around the tree, he saw his brother Zee standing there. Zee was also dressed like David. He was holding a four-foot hardwood branch in his hand. David stopped short, his chest heaving with trying to catch his breath. Both men looked at the camouflage-clad young woman lying on her back between them. A hard blow to the head had knocked her helmet off, exposing long dark brown curls and blood on the left side of her head. Zee felt her neck for a pulse.

"She is alive, but we need to get her to Doc Julikai right away."

Before helping to pick her up, David grabbed up the rifle and placed it between some large closely spaced branches. He used his strength and the rest of his adrenaline to crack the rifle in half. He grabbed the unconscious woman carefully supporting her head on his forearms. Zee led the way by holding her legs at the knees and started to walk back to the village.

"Thank you, Zee. You prevented me from killing this woman," David said.

Zee answered without turning around. "She was never in danger from you, my brother. She was already aiming her gun at the side of the tree that you would come from. This woman was certainly going to kill you today. However, you were a fine distraction, and together we prevented her from doing many bad things."

David looked down on the delicate features of the white woman's face, which was covered in camouflage makeup. He noticed that the side of her head was already starting to swell. He spoke softly to her. "Today you have a chance to change your life."

Left behind them as they walked toward the village was a broken rifle, a backpack full of gear, and David's pear-shaped double-edged knife. He had decided that he really never needed it and never would. Somewhere, Trevor, the guardian angel, was smiling.

"It is very good when an angel can be so proud of the people he protects," he said.

Julikai

Julikai grew up in Israel surrounded by a loving and supportive family. As a little girl, she found and cared for any creature wounded or sick so it was no surprise that she eventually ended up in the medical field. With each experience, she became even more committed to improve her professional care to help those in need.

The most difficult time of Julikai's life was during her mandatory two-year military service. While on patrol, she was ordered to protect a border area. Unexpectedly, a group of students was seen advancing toward her observation area. The order issued was to shoot to stop any "armed protestors."

Julikai, along with her fellow soldiers, aimed and discharged their weapons. The person running toward her fell. The few remaining protestors turned and fled back in panic. Julikai cautiously approached the body of the first person she had ever shot. Sickeningly, she looked into the sightless eyes of a young girl lying there in a pool of blood. Next to the body was a plank of wood that had been carved and painted to look like a gun. Putting her rifle down, Julikai turned and walked away, knowing she would never kill another human being. She was allowed to finish her term of service as a field medic. She knew she could never compensate for this horrible act of murder; rather, she would do all she could to focus on helping others to live.

After the army, Julikai put all her energy into learning more about traumatic injuries. She met a very old surgeon who wanted to travel to the very worst war-torn countries to treat victims of explosive effects. Old Dr. Kinder graciously accepted this very energetic young woman's offer to assist in these efforts. Travelling throughout Southeast Asia, Africa, the Middle East, and other lands, they treated the most desperately wounded victims. Finally, they arrived in the village where Julikai now lived. Dr. Kinder had contracted a fatal case of pneumonia. They had worked side by side for nearly nine years. For Julikai, it was as if she lost her best friend and mentor.

With his final breath, the old doctor said, "You will always have what you need to do the things you must do." He pointed toward the crate of surgical instruments and the stack of boxes filled with medical books, then silently slipped away.

Today Julikai was busy with her two patients both mercenary soldiers: Drayton, the merc who had tangled with the tripwires of an explosive booby trap, and Maxine who had been clubbed as she was trying to shoot one of the deminers. In spite of losing a hand and an eye, Drayton's recovery was progressing nicely. The left side of Maxine's head was badly swollen. She needed constant monitoring to avoid any permanent brain injury. Maxine jerked her arm away as Julikai was attempting to check her pulse.

"Good morning, Maxine," Drayton said to the injured soldier. "I haven't seen you since you parachuted out of the plane that brought us here."

"How are you feeling?" Julikai asked in her usual soothing tone.

Maxine neither responded to Drayton's comment nor Julikai's question. Her eyes widened from fear, and she demanded, "Am I a prisoner? Where am I?"

"You're temporarily out of commission," Drayton volunteered as he surveyed the young woman with his one good eye.

Ignoring Drayton's comments, Julikai answered Maxine, "You have sustained a very hard impact to the head. You must rest quietly so we can make sure you do not have any residual effect from this injury. You are not a prisoner. You are in our village field hospital. I believe that in time you will be fine."

Maxine then addressed Drayton who was still starring at her. "Where are my clothes, my gear?"

"Gone and very definitely, gone!" Drayton said with a large toothy grin. "Welcome to your new home for now."

Maxine proceeded to spew out some very foul curse words that surprised even Julikai.

Suddenly, the door to the hospital opened, and Dax entered. He went straight to Julikai and reported that the mercenaries have become mechanized. Taking a longer look at Julikai and seeing the tiredness in her eyes, he asked with concern, "Have you been sleeping lately?"

"Some," Julikai replied. Her long wavy hair was almost totally white which gave her a unique appearance of purity. She had a beautiful face with warm, caring brown eyes. "What makes you think they are mechanized?"

"Maria and Jacob were on the ridge when a merc tank hit a mine," Dax said. He anticipated her next question by saying that Maria and Jacob made it back to the village without a scratch. "I went up to the spot and found no survivors. It looks like the burnt surface of the moon."

"So what is the plan now that we have tanks coming toward us?" Julikai asked. "We have no weapons."

Dax smiled his confident grin and replied, "I am taking the deminers off their regular duties. They are already going out on bicycles with bags of sugar to stop the mercs."

Perplexed, Julikai asked Dax, "You are offering gifts to the mercs?"

"Gifts!" said Dax, chuckling. "That is such a lovely way to put it. The plan is very old school, you'll see."

"She flew the coup!" Drayton announced. Neither Dax nor Julikai noticed that Maxine had slipped out.

Julikai removed her lab coat and grabbed her field trauma pack. "She must be brought back here immediately. She is not ready to be up and about so soon after her injury."

"Need help?" Dax offered.

"She is my responsibility—my patient!" Julikai replied as she ran out the door.

"Just as I thought you would say," Dax replied. Then he yelled out to her, "Please be careful, Julie. We can't do without you!"

Tracking small barefoot prints for about an hour, Julikai spotted a woman fleeing far in the distance. The white hospital gown and bandage on her head identified the person as Maxine. The figure in white was running as fast as she could.

"Please, Trevor, let me bring her back," Julikai prayed to the guardian angel that she had only heard about but came to believe in.

Panic clouded Maxine's thoughts and actions. She had to get away but in which direction? She saw a tall, black primitive man in the distance. She heard Julikai calling her name. Fear made her run even faster. Suddenly, she fell. A sniper bullet caught her under the jaw and sent her body spinning like a white cloth in a strong wind.

Lying motionless on the ground, Maxine thought, *This really hurts!* The light around her began to fade quickly. Her glazed eyes remained open like a fallen deer. It was on that plain and at that moment Maxine died. She had been targeted as a villager by a fellow mercenary. The sniper mentally celebrated another kill and withdrew back deep inside a line of trees.

Julikai ran up to Maxine, throwing her trauma pack to the ground. She immediately tried to stop the bleeding while checking for a pulse. She tried chest compressions for almost thirty minutes with no result. Tears were streaming down her face as she looked into Maxine's empty eyes and saw another young woman from another time lying on the ground, shot and lifeless. Crying uncontrollably, she felt Dax's hand on her shoulder.

"You've done all you could, Julie," Dax said in a fatherly tone. "I think you are needed back at the hospital. Drayton may have a bit of infection. We should be heading back."

Julikai kept crying while Dax buried Maxine's body. He had to use his bayonet, the same tool he used to prod the ground in search of landmines. Once a weapon of war, it had become a tool of peace. Today it was a burial shovel. Just before dark, they began slowly walking back to the village together. No words were spoken, for each knew about death and loss.

Young Lincoln

A few times in your life, you may meet a young person who seems to possess wisdom far beyond their actual years. Sixteen-year-old Lincoln was one of those rare individuals.

The youngest deminer in the village, this red-haired, light-green-eyed young man was destined to make a positive impact on the world. He had drifted in to the village as an orphan from Lebanon. Both of his parents had died a horrible death from a major bombing campaign on Beirut, the capital city. It was after this bombing he witnessed many deaths and injuries, among them innocent children from ordnance that failed to function on impact. He decided that this was going to be one of his main passions in his life—to teach children what to do if they should ever be in this situation. When he had arrived in this particular village, he knew that this would be his new home. It was a place to prove himself as a man and to save lives. Clearly, Lincoln was well on his way to achieving both of these objectives.

The slightly built teenager coasted his bicycle into the center of the village. Lincoln was exhilarated at the success of his assigned mission. He had been tasked with finding some of the mercenary armored tanks and to disable them by adding sugar to the fuel tanks. Instead, Lincoln had a real stroke of luck by discovering two large refueling trucks. During the night, he managed to pour about twenty-five pounds of raw sugar into each large reservoir. During the next couple of days, this contaminated fuel would freeze the engines of any refueled assault vehicle.

Since he quickly completed his task, Lincoln was the first to return to the village. He now found himself with time on his hands while awaiting the return of the other deminers. He decided to visit the injured mercenary, Drayton, in the little field hospital. Lincoln had rescued Drayton from the mine field where he had landed and detonated a land mine.

Entering the hospital, he greeted Julikai, the field medic. Julikai appeared to be visibly upset. "Hey, Julie," Lincoln said cheerfully. "How's our patient? Say, didn't you have a woman merc here also?"

"She ran away and was killed on the plains by a sniper," Julikai said, averting her tearstained face. "I saw it happen and tried to help her, but she was already gone." Those last words trailed off sadly. "I am going to make some tea. Keep an eye on Drayton for me for a little while, will you?"

"Sure," Lincoln said as he walked over to the mercenary's bed. He knew Julikai felt bad and wished to console her, but she was a very private person.

Drayton was awake now and looked sideways at young Lincoln. "You look familiar. Have we met somewhere before?"

"I pulled you out of the minefield. Since I was the first to find you, I took charge of the rescue. Circumstances like that require a one-man operation. No need to risk a lot more casualties." He spoke as if he were reading a protocol from a textbook.

"Well, I guess I owe you." Drayton extended his left hand and motioned for Lincoln to take the large gold ring from his finger.

"Is that all your life is worth?" Lincoln questioned, looking into the man's eye.

"What then?" Drayton requested.

"Teach me what you know!" the teenager said in a firm voice. "If I understand how booby traps are placed, then I will be a much better deminer."

"Yeah, sure, whatever," Drayton responded in an uninterested manner.

"We start now," Lincoln ordered. "Let's go." Lincoln indicated for Drayton to get up.

Drayton's left eye had a crazed look. "Are you nuts? I am badly injured here."

"Do I need to carry you?" Lincoln said.

Without saying another word, Drayton stiffly moved to a sitting position on the side of the bed. Using the back of the chair near his bed, he steadied himself to a standing position. He had only been up and about for the past few days and still needed some assistance in getting around. "Where are we going?" he asked.

"Not far." Lincoln scribbled a quick note to Julikai, hoping that she would not be angry with him for taking Drayton to see Marcus. "We are going to see another landmine victim."

By the time they had walked the short distance to Marcus's house, Drayton was in serious pain. He said nothing. He refused to show this kid how badly he felt.

Marcus was sitting at the kitchen table. His facial bandages had been removed. It had been nearly a month since the blast, and he still looked awful. Maria and Jacob were out tending to some crops. Lincoln was pleased that the three of them would be alone in the small cottage.

"How are you doing today, Marcus?" Lincoln asked. Without waiting for a reply, he said, "This is Drayton. He is the merc that got injured parachuting into the minefield. He knows about booby traps and is going to give us the scoop on what we have in the field."

"My vision has come back pretty good," Marcus stated. "I'm lucky I didn't lose anything but blood." He noticed that Drayton had not been as fortunate with bandages on the stump of his right arm and over his sightless right eye socket. "What do you want with me?" Marcus asked.

"We need to figure out why you got hurt. What happened even though you were following the correct procedure. We have to make sense of your accident so it does not happen again," Lincoln explained.

"I have been playing that scenario over and over in my mind to try to figure out exactly what went wrong," Marcus said as Drayton and Lincoln took the two remaining chairs at the table.

"What were your actions before the mine exploded?" Drayton asked.

"Prodding with my old bayonet," Marcus explained. "I had located the mine with my metal detector and had just started prodding the ground. I was going deeper to make sure there was nothing underneath it."

"When we place the landmine, we try to guess what direction you will approach for prodding and angle the landmine that way," Drayton said calmly. "Then when you push a tool into the ground, the pressure plate is activated because it was aimed right at you. As you know, protecting the minefield from being cleared is part of our process."

"Makes sense to position them that way," Marcus said. "Sounds like that is what may have happened to me."

A long silence permeated the still air in the room as Drayton looked at Marcus's burned and disfigured face. His own wounds were aching in protest. He just wanted to get back to the hospital and lie down. He suddenly realized what terrible things people do to each other in war. Drayton looked at Marcus and said, "I'm really sorry, Marcus."

"Yeah, so am I. Like I said, it could have been a lot worse." Marcus continued, "Listen, it was gutsy of you to stop by, and I should probably say something cordial or even that I forgive you for being what you are…but I'm just not ready to do that yet."

"I wouldn't expect you would ever do that. Just keep getting better, all right?" Drayton slowly rose in quiet agony to leave.

"Yeah, same to you," Marcus replied.

"Well, that was helpful, Dray," Lincoln said. "Can you make your way back to the hospital? I want to stay and talk with Marcus for a little while."

"No problem," Drayton said. Slowly he made his way back to the hospital, hoping he would not collapse before he got there.

"We will meet here the same time tomorrow!" Lincoln yelled as Drayton began to slowly go through the doorway.

"I'll be here," Drayton replied. Without turning around, he raised his left hand in a feeble wave.

Maria came back with Jacob in tow. He pleaded with her to let him go out and play with some of his friends. Maria smiled and said, "Be careful and come back when you hear me call. We will have dinner then."

"OK, Mama!" Jacob ran out the door.

After a few minutes of chatting with Maria and Marcus, Lincoln left the cottage and decided to walk toward the sounds of the children playing. Watching the children playing always brought a smile to his face.

Children make the world a happier place to live, Lincoln thought.

As he came to the area, he stopped for a brief second and then realized that the children were playing far too close to the flags that indicated an unclear area. His breath caught as he saw one of the boys throw a ball to Jacob who was very near the hazardous markers. Luckily, Jacob caught the ball. He saw Lincoln and waved. Lincoln called the boys over to him watching them carefully.

"Hey, guys, I want you to look back at the area where you were playing. What do you see?" Lincoln asked.

They all turned around and looked toward their playing area. One of the older boys said "Oops! We were too close to the flags and near the danger area."

One of the other boys said, "Lincoln, come see what we found. We would have brought it to you, but since you are here, come see."

They all started going over to where they had been playing.

"Hang on, just point to where you were. I will find whatever you had seen. I want you all far back to a very safe distance. Wait for me at the field hospital," Lincoln said as he pointed to the large white building in the distance.

The oldest boy pointed to the general area of concern. Then, they all ran back toward the field hospital, leaving Lincoln to check it out. Lincoln walked up to the edge of the flagged area. He easily spotted a rusted dome-shaped object. It appeared to be about the size of a baseball.

"Cluster bomb," Lincoln said out loud. He pulled out strips of red ribbon to tie around the border flag closest to the item in question. A recent rain had probably uncovered the dirt that had been covering it. He looked for any other suspicious objects but saw there were none. He marked his map of the village area so he could report the item for disposal.

Lincoln went back to where the children were waiting for him. He told them that they had done the right thing by not touching the piece of metal. "You told me right away, and that was another good thing to do."

Little Jacob spoke up, "And then, you kept us from going back to the danger area."

"Right you are, little guy," Lincoln responded. "You will all make great deminers someday. Right now, you are the very best safety kids I know."

The children were all beaming and smiling proudly at what they had done.

Lincoln was smiling too. He was also very relieved that the children had not been injured.

"Let's go over the three *R*s again, OK?" Lincoln said to the group. "Recognize—anything that looks unusual. Do not touch it. Retreat—walk away bringing anyone who is there with you. Report—Go tell one of the deminers. Remember that unexploded ordnance can be anywhere so be careful."

In the distance, the sound of Maria's voice could be heard.

Jacob said, "Gotta go. Supper is ready." He waved good-bye to Lincoln. All the other boys ran off for home too.

Lincoln squared his shoulders as he went to Mama Ha's cottage. She would have something amazing to eat right about now. He felt his parent's pride within himself. They were surely watching him, and they were happy.

Sugar to Trade

In the quiet of the day the sound of galloping could be heard. The sound came from bicycle tires rolling and bouncing over a bed of sharp gray rocks alongside abandoned railroad tracks. Dax rode the rusty old bicycle steadily on. He would sometimes coast to rest but never sat on the bicycle seat. It was much too rough a ride for sitting. Giant trees grew over the tracks presenting a long corridor to travel ahead.

Sunbeams streamed down all around him as Dax started thinking about the other deminers he had sent on an important mission. They were to infiltrate the mercenary campsites to place sugar in as many vehicle fuel tanks as possible. If successful, the enemy soldiers would be greatly inhibited from advancing their killing spree. As he was much older and slower than the others, he felt his efforts should be placed in another direction.

Dax was pedaling toward a distant village with four bags of sugar for trading. He figured the destination was about twenty miles away when his front tire blew out. He stopped to examine the flat tire. There was no way the rotted tube could be patched. He went to work stuffing dry grass into the old tire. From countless years of bike repair experience, he felt that this was the logical option. After a lot of grunting and packing, the tire was "inflated" enough to ride on.

It was good to be alone. Time riding a bike helped clear his mind and think about future possibilities. He knew that without a doubt, the attacks by the mercenaries would increase and become worse. Maybe if there was some way their pay could be interrupted. If this could be accomplished, surely the mercs would pull back their efforts. Dax pondered some creative ways of making this plan effective.

By midafternoon, Dax saw that he was approaching a clearing in the trees. He was nearing Tranquility, an important village of trade for the entire region. His thoughts shifted to trading the bags of sugar. It should be something the whole village could use. They all needed a boost to their spirits and a reward for their hard work. Rum, he thought, but realized it was a selfish wish and not everyone drinks. As he dismounted and walked his bicycle onto the dusty main street, he thought of just the right "present." He would trade for coffee and present it to Julikai. No one worked harder or deserved it more than she. Giving a gift to her would be the same as giving it to the whole village, for she shared all she had with everyone.

As he propped the bicycle against the closest building, Dax surveyed the little town. The wooden store fronts gave the appearance of a miniature old west town. Everywhere, people were busy hauling merchandise around in handcarts. Near each doorway, a cheerful store clerk could be heard singing and advertising what was to be found inside for trade. Tranquility had survived many wars in the past without ever being attacked. It was too important and needed by everyone in order for survival. Even mercenaries seldom caused problems here. They felt a civilized place to hang out was a necessity while being deployed. The exceptions to this rule were the occasional ruthless individuals.

Several buildings away, Dax noticed a large sign with huge letters: COFFEE. At the very same time, he spotted Trevor across the street. The dark-skinned angel was shaking his head trying to stop Dax from entering the store. Dax pretended to not see the Aboriginal who looked out of place amongst all of the merchandise and activity.

"I'll be in, out, and on my way in no time flat," Dax rationalized out loud. He tried to ignore this obvious warning of danger. "Life is too short to live in fear. Besides, this is the only place that trades with coffee."

He entered the coffee shop. Inside it was cool and shady with streaks of sunlight filtering through the cracks in the wooden walls. An older woman gave Dax a warm smile. She made an even exchange and gave Dax four bags of coffee beans for his four bags of sugar. He was invited to sit down and enjoy a free cup of coffee and a scone. It was the custom in Tranquility to offer a gift to travelers after a trade had been completed. Dax sat down at one of the many thick wooden tables. It reminded him of visiting someone's home kitchen a very long time ago.

After taking his first bite of the delicious scone and a sip of strong black coffee, he became aware of the other customers. Three mercenaries were staring at him from the table in the corner. The three men were laughing and pointing at him. Dax could see a bottle of rum on the table. Each man had a rifle, barrel side up leaning against their thighs.

The largest man stood grabbing his rifle by the barrel sight and started to walk toward Dax. Dax watched the man approach him. He had a scruffy beard, shaved head, and skull tattoos on each arm. The only color on his camouflage uniform was the purchased service medals and a long blood-red scarf around his neck. The jungle boots stomped against the wood planked floor as he came nearer. His foul breath smelled like some dead animal. He bent over to inspect the patch on Dax's right shirt sleeve. The embroidered patch was the international symbol for unexploded ordnance: a simple silhouette of an aerial bomb bordered by a triangle with rounded corners. Above the symbol was only one word: DEMINER.

"Well, if it isn't one of those little cowardly deminer dudes who refuse to carry a weapon," the merc growled. His friends started chuckling.

Dax put his coffee down slowly and watched the man without looking directly into his eyes. Every muscle tensed as he noticed the mercenary's rifle starting to rise up slowly.

"Not a good day for you to be out without a weapon, wimp!" growled the stinky voice as he raised his rifle higher.

Dax knew the bully meant to use the rifle on the deminer's head. Potentially, this could very well be a deathblow. He knew whatever was going to happen would be soon.

In one motion, Dax grabbed the blood-red scarf and with every bit of stored energy in his body yanked it far down past the edge of the table. The big man's face landed flat against the hard tabletop. The merc slid and collapsed backward in a heap of camouflage fabric.

Calmly Dax rose to his feet and collected his bags of coffee and walked slowly to the door. He could hear the unconscious man's breath gurgling with blood from his facial wound. The other two mercenaries were caught off guard. They attempted to reach for their rifles which fell and clattered to the floor. They decided they would remain seated, not wishing to look more stupid after this clumsy failed attempt.

Dax slowly walked through the doorway, apologizing to the store's owner as he left. He half expected one of the other mercenaries to shoot him in the back, but a bullet never came.

The old deminer went back to his bicycle and tied the bundles of coffee on the back rack. He took off along the dirt path through the trees toward his own village. No more open spaces along the railroad tracks for him today. He had people who would be depending on him back home. There would be no more tempting fate and no more ignoring warnings from a guardian angel.

"I wonder if you had anything to do with those rifles falling to the floor. If so, thanks, Trevor," Dax said out loud.

The old man's stiff and tired body mounted the rusty bicycle. Dax pedaled briskly down the dirty trail. The dust from the rotten bike tires rose, and when it cleared, there was no sign of him.

Management Trouble

It was only 10:00 a.m., and the sun was already creating another steamy day for those sitting around the hotel pool. Six men in shorts and aloha shirts were under an umbrella that was shading a fiberglass table. The waiter had just replenished their drinks. Nothing but the best for this group of managers for they were in charge of various groups of men working to conquer this region. Lavish accommodations were one of the many perks of the management jobs.

Paul, the newest member of this group, was leading this morning's conversation. "How can we send in mercenaries without any medical backup plan? What happens to them if they encounter resistance from hostile local militia?" Paul was asking with genuine concern on his face, for he was the safety officer for the project. He felt personally responsible for each of the mercenaries who were in the field.

"The same reason that we sent in tanks with no mechanical support and no spare parts," Mike replied. He was a tan athletic-looking man with gray wavy styled hair. "The more money we hold back, the larger our bonus when the job is completed. Besides, this project is only supposed to last fifteen days tops."

"Still, how would you like to be out there with no logistical support, no backup, and no evacuation plan?" Paul protested.

Roger, a red-faced accountant with delicate features, gave his opinion. "Look, they are mercenaries. They get paid more than four times the wages of a regular army soldier. They know the risks, and they are well compensated for any hazards they might encounter."

"Oh, and you are telling us this because of your vast experience in the field?" Mike responded sarcastically.

The other three men agreed with Roger regarding the fate of the mercenaries. None of them had any notion of what the people in the field did nor did they ever care to know. Quick results and ample paychecks were their only motivations.

"It just seems like a half-baked plan with too many loose ends," Paul continued. "Has anyone heard how we're doing? We are what now, eleven days in?"

"All I know is that there has been limited communication from the field," Mike answered. "We have two helicopters doing recon. They should have reported back by now."

Roger looked up and saw Tim, the project manager, heading their way. "Well, here comes the boss-man now. I have a feeling he is about to tell us how things are going, and he doesn't look too happy."

The project manager was walking toward them, looking particularly agitated today. He greeted them by slamming his fist on the edge of the table, causing some glasses and bottles to fall. "Meeting! Penthouse! Now!" Tim demanded. He turned around and headed back toward the elevator. He did not bother to look to see if anyone followed. The group just looked at him in bewilderment and watched him move into the hotel lobby. A couple of them started to snicker. The sudden appearance of Tim in the daylight was indeed quite comical. From his flowered shirt, red bald head, and an even redder bulbous nose, Tim looked more like a disheveled clown rather than someone who was in charge of a multimillion-dollar assault mission.

The men decided that they better get moving. By the time they all reached the penthouse, Tim had changed into a dress shirt and tie.

"This looks serious," Mike said under his breath to Roger.

"I was very clear when I said *no cell phones* were to be taken into the field!" Tim was yelling. "Now the mercs have found out that they would not be getting any money until the mission is completed. Many of them are wondering if we are going to pay them at all. Some are leaving the job. There is even a possibility that some of them actually caused the breakdown of the armored vehicles! The end result is that little progress has been made in getting the farmers to leave their lands." While Tim was ranting, his skin color was changing from crimson to an odd shade of purple.

The one subject which attracted the men's attention most was the possibility of not getting paid. One by one, they took out their smart phones to check their bank statements. They wanted to make sure that they had been getting their direct deposits into their accounts on schedule.

At this new distraction, Tim was working himself into a full-blown fit of rage. He was shaking as he raised his right fist in the air and continued to yell. He was so focused on what he wanted to say next that he ignored the fact that he could no longer raise his left arm.

"Well, we still have a large budget!" Tim screamed. "I've ordered a full-scale airstrike. Tomorrow, I'm going to bomb all those idiots back to the Stone Age!"

Paul was shocked by the announcement of this latest strategy. "What about all of the mercenaries who are still in the field. There is not sufficient time left for them to get out!"

"It will serve them right for not getting the job done fast in the first place!" Tim said, putting his right hand on his chest. He started coughing, then gasping for air. His already big eyes were bulging. Drops of sweat seemed to leap off his purple head.

Paul, Mike, and Roger were feeling sick at the news of an air strike. For the first time, the reality of killing was coming home to them. Paul thought to himself, *This is insane. Why did I ever get involved with this project?*

The other three men were already leaving the penthouse. None of the managers had been paid, and they wanted to find out why.

Tim suddenly grabbed his chest and collapsed on the floor. Paul rushed to kneel by Tim's motionless body. He yelled to Mike and Roger to call for help. He began chest compressions and continued until the paramedics arrived. Thanks to Paul's efforts, the paramedics were able to stabilize Tim. Tim was placed on a stretcher and loaded into an ambulance for transport to a hospital.

Paul felt emotionally and physically exhausted. He no longer wanted to be associated with this organization, which cared so little for human life. He decided that he would write his letter of resignation and send it off right away. He would be done with this dirty business once and for all. Perhaps he could find a way to effect a better change to the existing situation if that were even possible at this point.

Two hundred miles away, bombs were being loaded onto several aircraft. Pilots and their crewmembers were plotting tomorrow's mission. Red triangles had been placed on the charts. Each red triangle marked the location of a village to be bombed.

The Approaching Storm

The sound of a rattling bicycle could be heard as it was approaching the village. Dax was pedaling on a nearly flat front tire as he rode between cottages. The old deminer was surprised to see Drayton walking around outside the field hospital. The bike slid sideways as it came to a stop. A wide spray of dirt flew toward the feet of the injured mercenary.

"So you are feeling good enough to get around?" Dax asked Drayton with a grin.

"It's really a form of forced physical therapy," Drayton replied, rolling his left eye up to the sky. "I left the hospital with young Lincoln to visit Marcus. When I came back, Julikai had remade my bed and said, 'You've been released from the hospital. Now go finish healing.' So I have been wandering around trying to figure out where I can stay."

"You can bunk at my place until you build your own cottage," Dax said, still chuckling over Julikai's orders to Drayton. "Do you want to see something beautiful?"

"Sure," Drayton responded. He had never built anything in his life and was trying to imagine how he could possibly create an actual building.

"Follow me," Dax said as he pulled one end of a cord releasing four bags of coffee beans from the bicycle frame. The bike crashed to the ground. Drayton noticed the front tire. It was rotten and spotted with tear holes with a lot of dry grass oozing out.

Dax let Drayton enter the field hospital first so the mercenary could see Julikai's face when she saw her gift.

Turning around from her medical studies, Julikai was about to ask Drayton if he was experiencing any problems from his injuries. She spotted the bags of coffee Dax held. Instantly, she flashed the most incredible and gorgeous smile that Drayton had ever seen. He had thought her quite good looking, but now he was entirely taken over by the sight of her. He was glad he did not have to say anything as he would have risked sounding like a blabbering idiot.

"That can't be just for me!" Julikai said, still beaming and smelling the delightful aroma of coffee beans.

"No one deserves it more, Julie," Dax said. "Perhaps you could share a few pots of coffee during our meeting today."

"Gladly. Thank you so much!" Julikai then left to try to find a way to grind the beans.

Dax noticed a goofy smile on Drayton's face. Dax thought, *Oh, so that's how it is*. And he said to Drayton, "Not a gnats chance in Hades!"

Drayton was embarrassed. Dax seemed to be able to read his mind, but still he wondered if he had any chance to get to know Julikai better.

"We have a meeting to organize right away," Dax said, moving Drayton's thoughts away from Julikai.

The rumor of coffee soon made everyone in the village gather together quickly. The farmers came in from the fields. The deminers who had only just returned from their sabotage mission were yawning and stumbling toward the central area of the compound.

Dax felt sure about the likelihood of an air strike. The vision of it had recently come to him in a dream. He knew that a plan of survival had to be formulated soon.

Mama Ha began serving soup as the last of the women and children gathered around. Dax was letting everyone eat and sip coffee before speaking to the villagers. He was as close to a leader as they had in this tiny remote community. Smiling, Mama Ha handed out warm flat bread as she watched the villagers enjoy her cooking. When everyone had finished eating and chatting amongst themselves, the entire village became very quiet.

Dax stepped forward relating all he had heard from people along his trade journey. "The snipers had not yet appeared to be causing an extreme amount of casualties. The recent efforts of putting sugar in the fuel tanks would slow the threat of armored vehicles. The real question now: What will come at us next?"

Drayton recently had a dream of Trevor shouting one word over and over. "Bombies!" Drayton shouted out shocked by the sound and urgency of his own voice. "If this invasion force can afford it, carpet bombing with cluster bombs is the next logical step."

A gasp of pure shock was heard from the gathering. It was the worst possible scenario.

"Well, we just have to leave!" Maria said. "We have to clear out now. Even if we survive the bombing, our land will be contaminated for years, probably decades. Many of those bombies will remain to pose a danger like unexploded landmines. They will be everywhere!"

Drayton stood up and addressed the crowd. "We probably would not have time to evacuate. Even if we did, how can we be certain that we would be outside of the bombing area. We need to find a place within the vicinity that would be safe for us all. Don't you have some kind of cave nearby?"

Surprise at this suggestion appeared on a number of faces. They wondered how Drayton knew about the cave. No one ever spoke of it. It was the place where the villagers stored food and supplies. No one would have said anything about this secret place to an enemy mercenary. While he exhibited a small attempt to become a part of the village, he had not yet earned their trust.

"I heard a voice say to go to the cave in a dream a couple of nights ago," Drayton said without any hesitation.

There was a momentary hush that fell over the entire crowd. Finally, Dax spoke with authority and confidence. "We move everyone and everything that we can to the large cave starting now!"

Without any word of protest, everyone started to disband and to move what essential things they could to the cave.

As an afterthought, Dax added, "Let's put a deadline of six hours to be there and be ready!"

Drayton, although still in a lot of pain from his wounds, went straight to the field hospital. Julikai would be in need of his help. The entire medical operation must be relocated into the cave. She could not refuse his offer. Mama Ha was near the field hospital watching them both as they began packing. Nodding her head and smiling, she recognized that a partnership bond had already started between them.

Young Lincoln fashioned a kind of cart with wooden boards and two bicycles. He and the other deminers ran supplies to the cave just outside of the village. Everyone moved with great efficiency and purposefulness. There would be plenty of time to rest after the bombing started.

Early the next day, Lincoln was taking his turn to watch for any signs of the attack. From the top of the hill, he had a good view of the surrounding countryside. In the distance, he saw clouds of dust, and it was heading in their direction. As the dust cleared, he saw people coming. He recognized a number of people from a neighboring village. They too had a forewarning of what was to come. Although the quarters would be tight, there would be no purpose in discussing whether or not to allow them to share the cave's protection. Everyone who was concerned for their survival was part of this large and expanding family.

The teenage boy was looking wistfully upon the approaching people. "Should we survive the bombing, how soon could we manage to return to a normal life? We will lose all of our crops and everything that we have built here. What will starting over look like?" Lincoln stood up and dusted off his clothes. He went to inform the others that company was coming. A fresh warm wind was beginning to blow in from the west. It felt to Lincoln like an ancient symbol of warning.

A Very Dark Day

Preparing a large cave as a combination bomb shelter and refugee camp was no easy task. However, with dozens of willing volunteers, each needed task was quickly accomplished. An area was designated for meals assembly, another area for sleeping, and further away toilet facilities were dug out and engineered for proper sanitation. These details kept Dax busy, but a much more important problem was worrying his mind. Cluster bombs were often used in war to pierce armor. In civilian applications, the same principals were employed for drilling through rock in commercial mining. Could the thickness of the cave's ceiling withstand a long barrage of these molten jets of energy?

"Enough!" Dax said to himself. This train of thought was pointless. There were no other options available. It was a futile exercise to estimate the thickness of the cave's overhead ceiling. This was the only place to be, and he needed to be thankful for it.

Dax went over to Marcus to discuss what they could do in advance of the siege. "Sandbags are needed by the entrance to protect the villagers from fragmentation. How can we set this up?"

"Lincoln suggested using T-shirts with the neck and sleeves tied up then filling them with sand or dirt," Marcus replied.

"Brilliant!" Dax exclaimed. "We need about six bags deep for frag protection. What about deflecting the blast energy from the explosions?"

"Wooden wall sections cut from the sides of our cottages," Marcus answered. "We will lay them diagonally, like shingles on a roof, backfilling with sandbags to complete the makeshift shield."

"What do you reckon is our next major obstacle?" Dax asked.

"Space is our biggest problem right now. When the other villagers arrived, we increased our population requiring a lot more space. We also need to assess the ventilation in the cave," Marcus said. "Hopefully, the bombing raids will not last long, or maybe there will be an interval between air strikes allowing us to temporarily remove a small bit of the shielding."

"Yep, we will do whatever we need to do. You are doing a great job, Marcus!" Dax responded with a smile of pride.

"It will be a good job if we all make it through this safely," Marcus stated in a serious tone.

To help keep up spirits and energy, Mama Ha and a German woman named Gelda from the neighboring village took over the "kitchen." They made friends quickly preparing soup and flat bread in a jury rigged kitchen just to the right of the cave's entrance. Tirelessly, these two mismatched women put an amazing meal together as they fed everyone. Mama Ha, with her slight but sturdy frame, passed out the meals, while Gelda chopped vegetables and frequently stirred the soup. This pair of cooks worked like a well-oiled machine even though neither one of them spoke the other's language. Smiles and nods were their means of communication, which appeared to be all they needed.

As night was falling, everyone became physically exhausted. Soon, the cave became very quiet except for the occasional stirring of its inhabitants. The men were taking shifts outside on a scheduled rotation. A lookout was always posted on the top of the hill, which was the cave's rooftop.

It was late and dark when Maria suddenly awakened, not knowing where she was. She did know that she was not in her bed in her home, and the unknown frightened her. She felt Marcus next to her, but where was Jacob? She started calling her little boy's name when Marcus raised her head and kissed her forehead. He told her that they were in a safe cave and that Jacob was on his other side sound asleep. Reality came back to her. Everyone from the village and others were now in a cave, seeking shelter from a potential bombing that could happen at any time. What is going to happen to them? Will they be able to go back to their village? Would it even be there after all this? So many questions and there were no answers. Then she remembered the metal dragon and the feeling she had as they escaped and ran back to Marcus. They were safe as long as they were together as a family: Marcus, Jacob, and her. She started to settle back down beside Marcus when she felt a funny fluttery feeling in her abdomen. She hoped that she was not getting sick. She said a little prayer of thanks for being together and another prayer for protection in the coming days. As soon as she closed her eyes, she slept.

Very early the next morning, Julikai was already at work and starting to show some obvious signs of stress. Drayton, who was by her side, became very concerned.

"Are you all right? Do you really want to put these instruments with your books? Wouldn't they be better with the medical supplies?" Drayton asked.

"I've never been through a bombing raid," Julikai said with her voice trembling. "I don't know what to expect or how bad it will get."

"This will be my first bombing as a target," Drayton responded with a confident smile. "It can get as bad as it is possible to get, but we will all make it through this all right." Drayton took her hand and gently squeezed. He was surprised that she did not pull her hand away.

"Please stay with me through this." Julikai raised her eyes to look into his. "I'll be fine if you talk me through it."

"I will stay right here with you. And together, we will help wherever we are needed," Drayton answered.

Finally, Julikai withdrew her hand, saying, "People depend on me to be strong when they need me."

"I understand and you will be," said Drayton. They exchanged a warm glance.

Suddenly, their expressions changed when they heard David's loud warning coming from the top of the hill. "It's happening! Take cover!" In the distance, the African man could see clearly through binoculars. Small cigar shapes were falling down through the clouds. He noticed some of them seeming to momentarily hang in midair before they burst open dispensing cluster bombs, which rained down over the area. He jumped to his feet and hastily followed two other men rushing into the mouth of the cave. Frantically, they began packing the remaining sandbags into the last small gap in the cave's opening. In the darkness, everyone settled in to sit and wait.

Young children who had at first been excited to camp with the entire village were starting to cry. Fear of the unknown permeated the villagers. Everyone was clinging to each other and praying for safety. The approach of thousands of smaller explosions joined together creating loud bangs. When the bombs started to fall directly overhead, individual pops and cracks could not be discerned through the deafening roar.

Would the sandbags hold against flying fragmentation? Would the ceiling be worn away from the waves of shaped charges constantly bombarding it? These thoughts and more were running through Dax's mind. Suddenly, deep within his concentration, a voice could be heard. "No worries mate! She'll be right." It could only be Trevor, that guardian angel who calmed and protected them. "Yeah, it has to be," Dax muttered to himself.

For seven minutes, though it seemed more like three hours, the bombing continued. Remarkably the noise appeared to be diminishing. At first, Dax thought it was one of those rare episodes when his hearing would decrease and even go away completely for a couple of seconds. He knew that this was not the case when he clearly heard little Jacob shout out, "Wow, that was a really *big dragon*!" When she heard her son mention the dragon, it made Maria laugh nervously.

"Is anyone hurt? Please check the people around you!" Marcus's shout echoed back to those in the rear of the cave. Light from the candles, as they were lit, dimly illuminated the interior. The air was mixed with clouds of dust and dirt that had been shaken loose from the walls and overhead.

"Stay put. We will come to you!" It was Drayton speaking now as he and Julikai started moving among the coughing crowd. Amazingly, no one was injured. Julikai smiled as she saw Mama Ha rocking a three-month-old baby girl. She had a serene look on her face as she softly sang a lullaby where every word was "Ha." This old Vietnamese woman had been through countless bombings. She would never be used to these intrusions on life, but she would never succumb to the fear that they generated.

In the flickering candlelight, Julikai tenderly touched the old woman's face. A sense of calm descended upon the field medic's expression that was soon replaced by tears of appreciation and gratitude. In her mind, she voiced a simple prayer, "Thank God."

Through small spaces between the shifted sandbags smoke from burnt plants and spent explosives drifted inside. As a fresh breeze dissipated the dark noxious gasses, small beams of bright sunlight began to pierce deep inside of the cave. Everyone became silent as a new feeling of peace and hope began stirring within them.

Rebirth

It had been two hours since the last explosions were heard. The stillness that remained was somewhat unsettling. It was decided that everyone stay put for a while just to make sure a second wave of bombing did not occur. Often aircraft runs would be staggered to target anyone who comes out to retrieve casualties.

Most of the people remained in their places talking in low voices. Jacob and several other children had long abandoned their orders to remain quiet. They started a game of hide and seek while the older children sang some of their favorite songs. The cheerfulness of their young voices was a comfort to all.

Life goes on, Dax thought. To Dax, who had been so close to dying so many times in his life, this was a common occurrence. More than a continuation of old routines, he knew that this would be the start of a fresh new life for everyone. When people survive a tragedy together, a strong bond of kinship is created. Any new challenge would be faced together as a large and strong family unit. He looked back into the shelter seeing flickering candlelight and the faces of all the survivors. "It's now time to begin," he said in a voice just above a whisper.

Dax got up and, along with David, removed a small portion of the doorway shield allowing fresh air to circulate into the cave. Patterns of dust could be seen floating in the fresh air. Not knowing what was destroyed and where ordnance was dropped troubled his mind. He viewed the desolation of their beloved village. Failed ordnance items would be out there still lethal. Clearing the land needed to start at the entrance of their cave and gradually fan out from there. "We will reclaim our village," Dax muttered. It seemed that they had waited long enough. It was time to take a long look at their devastated old landscape. Now it was time to plan what must be done to carve a new life out of the unknown explosive contamination.

"Marcus," Dax yelled, "come to the entrance to look and help clear the entrance."

"Can I see too?" spoke up little Jacob as he followed his father to the front of the cave.

"Sure you can," Dax said. Dax picked up Jacob so he too could peek outside with his father.

Everyone was getting excited, stretching and talking with those around them. It would be a relief to get out of this cramped space. It was good hearing the activity and conversations after what had seemed to be such a long time of anticipation. Marcus held up his hands, letting them know that there was still danger out there, and they would not be leaving the confines of the cave right away. "Please be patient. We don't know what unexploded ordnance is left after the air raid. You all know that the exterior must first be cleared before anyone can step outside." The reality of the situation descended upon them though it did not dampen their spirits. They cleared the land and had made a living before the bombing, and they could do it all again.

Marcus and Dax continued to open up the doorway. "Take it slow and easy," Dax warned. "There could be sharp frag or possibly a bombie embedded in the sand bags."

"Zee. David. Lincoln. Bring up five metal detectors," Dax ordered.

Bright sunlight was now blinding Dax and Marcus. Soon, an opening was big enough for Marcus to climb up and take in a proper view. What he saw made him gasp. Their village below was completely gone except for perhaps two buildings. All around the trees had been broken into sharp wooden fans. Only a few limbs had leaves fluttering in the light breeze like tiny flags of surrender.

The expected smell of freshly detonated explosives reached Marcus's nose. Then the acrid smell of some kind of incendiary material came through the air. Lines of smoke appeared to be rising from odd places in the ground. When he raised his head a little higher, he could see the sugarcane fields completely engulfed in flames.

"The cane is burning!" Marcus reported. He decided to choose his future words more carefully so as not to cause alarm from those who could hear him. "We have a lot of work ahead of us" was all Marcus could say.

It was decided that all of the deminers would help to enlarge the cave's opening. They would prestack the sandbags in case the entrance would need to be quickly resealed in the event of another assault. Carefully they removed the wooden frames taken from their cottages and stacked them. Knowing how anxious people were, some of them were allowed to come up and view the former village area. There were not many comments among the observers, only the occasional curse word would slip out.

Dax envied Lincoln's energy as the young man hefted each sandbag and swung it in place. "I just can't remember what it was like to be that young," Dax said with a grin and a chuckle. All of the other men laughed as they too thought back to their youth. It felt good to laugh. Laughing assured them that this was real life and not just some weird dream. Children came up to see what was going on. They too smiled and laughed even though they did not fully understand what was so funny.

Lincoln switched on a metal detector, running it through its operational checks. He began sweeping the search head outside the entrance to the cave. "I feel as though I am leaving the womb for the first time," he said profoundly.

"Don't cry, baby," Marcus said. This caused everyone to join in a new round of raucous laughter.

"Julie, come quick. You've got to see this," Lincoln shouted in amazement.

Julikai and Drayton made their way to the entrance with Mama Ha right behind them.

"The field hospital is still there!" Julikai said as if she could not believe her own eyes. Drayton just looked at Julikai, caught up in her jubilation, and said, "Amazing." He could not take his eyes away from her and continued to smile. She noticed him looking at her. Blushing, she turned away but continued to smile. Drayton put his hand on Julikai's shoulder. "This is a very good sign, Julie!"

Julikai's eyes were now squinting as she looked back at him, knowing that he was testing to see if she would allow him to use her nickname. "Yes, I would say that it is a very good sign!" she said, still smiling.

Mama Ha looked down at the field hospital and a long sigh of "Ha" seemed to complete her contented face.

Using the metal detectors, the deminers removed several pounds of metal bomb fragments. They cleared a perimeter around the front of the entrance and marked the edge of the areas with flags. It wasn't a huge space but enough for people from the inside to come out and get a break from their confinement.

Gelda and Mama Ha set up their makeshift kitchen where it had been before. By dusk, soup was ready. Dax decided that this was enough activity for one day. Tonight everyone would rest. Tomorrow they would clear out a few more feet. Within a week or two, they hoped to be all the way to the village boundary. Rebuilding their way of life had officially begun.

The next morning, as Dax was looking over the jumbled mass of crushed trees and splintered remains of the cottages, he planned the first full day of clearance. In the hazy light, he noticed a dark figure of a one-legged man leaning on the outside of the field hospital. It was Trevor looking back and smiling. "You have been with us the whole time haven't you, my old friend?" Dax asked.

Suddenly, a strange and rare sensation of fear arrived like an electrical shock in Dax's body. It was the thumping sound of a helicopter far away. It seemed to be getting louder quickly. Several men who had also heard it arrived from inside the cave, ready to reseal the entrance with sandbags.

Marcus yelled frantically to Dax, "What's happening? Are they coming back to finish us off?"

Fear was threatening to replace hope.

Operation Lost Puppy

The pulsing beat of helicopter blades grew steadily louder. Was this another shipment of mercenaries? Could it be more airborne weaponry sent to kill any survivors of yesterday's bombing run? These were the thoughts going through the minds of the villagers as they ran back into the cave seeking shelter. Panic was clearly written on everyone's face. All talk stopped as they awaited the outcome of this latest sense of dread.

Lincoln, Zee, and David were restacking sandbags to close up the entrance. Dax, Drayton, and Marcus had their eyes glued to the sky trying to decipher the direction where the sound was coming from.

"Hold on," Drayton exclaimed, holding his hand out. "I know this sound. It's from a twin-bladed Russian or Czech helicopter. It's not a large gunship, and I don't think it's a troop transport either. I know I have heard this chopper before." Drayton strained to hear some other telltale characteristics for confirmation. "I don't remember exactly what it's called, but the United Nations employs it for some of their missions."

"Are you sure?" Marcus asked. "It's getting a little late for us to try to seal up the cave for the necessary protection!"

"Yes, I'm sure. I just can't figure out what the UN would be doing way out here," Drayton spoke while quizzically looking upward.

All three men watched as the large white helicopter approached. As it came over a hill, the two big distinctive letters were visible on its side—UN. Within minutes, it was hovering over the remnants of the village. It slowly landed just north of the field hospital building. A large sectional hatch came open from the right side of the chopper. Cables held the hatch as it swung to within inches of the ground. The engines shut down, and all that could be heard was the sound of the rotor blades as they slowly reduced rotating.

Dax and the others were staring in disbelief at what was happening. It just was not possible for that chopper to land among all the scattered live cluster bombs that were sure to be lying about. How did they know where to land without exploding them? To their amazement, several men wearing khaki uniforms with blue berets on their heads filed out. Each man held metal detectors, a type not recognizable by any of the deminers. One man followed them appearing to be the man in charge.

Dax shouted to the men below and waved his arms. The group looked upward at the cave. All of them waved back talking excitedly to each other. The man in charge held up his hand to stop any of the villagers from coming forward. He signaled that his crew would come to the villagers.

The group of United Nations Deminers worked their detectors in a careful sweeping motion as they advanced from the chopper. While they swept the ground with these instruments, they would occasionally plant a red survey flag into the ground. On each side of the line of men yellow survey flags were planted to designate the boundary of the path being cleared.

Marcus spoke first. "Well, I'll be…They are making a clear path from their chopper right to us. But how can they move so quickly. How did they find a spot that was clear enough to land? This is all very strange!" Both Drayton and Dax agreed. They had never seen men advancing so quickly while marking and clearing a path. They all waited anxiously to talk with these men of the UN.

Dax called out in a rare moment of total authority. "Gear up! Let's help them out. Bring out all our detectors and get to sweeping!"

Holding flags to mark possible unexploded ordnance positions, Dax encouraged his men to carefully swing their search instruments close but not touching the ground. "Watch your intervals and overlap your sweep patterns!" Occasionally, a deminer would pause and raise his hand. Dax would give him four red flags to be placed around the suspected explosive item lying on or below the ground.

Dax's crew worked methodically. However, they were moving at a snail's pace compared to the advancing United Nations team. Dax could hear their leader barking orders. "He's a Brit for sure!" Dax said out loud.

The UN deminers had traveled up the hill and covered nearly two hundred meters in a little over an hour. When both teams met, Dax's team had swept less than fifteen meters.

"Colonel Meadows at your service," a tall thin man with hazel eyes and a short cropped white moustache announced.

"Dax, the senior manager here" was the reply when the two men shook hands.

"How in the world were you able to do your search so fast?" Dax asked.

"Right! It's a brilliant little process that started out as a protocol called Operation Lost Puppy," the colonel replied. "You see, all of this aerial ordnance has been microchipped. Our detectors locate the item. Its location is GPS recorded. Then, we refer to a data base to tell us what the item is and how best to render it safe. Look at these serial numbers on the screen of this detector. These represent individual pieces of ordnance."

"This is brilliant," said Drayton who had walked from the cave to join the group. "How did you know this bombing raid used microchipped munitions?"

"The shipment of bombs that was purchased for this air raid mission was easily traced back to manufacturers who had adopted the Lost Puppy tagging protocol," the colonel explained.

"I remember several years ago a group of deminers had gotten together and discussed the archaic way everyone was locating and identifying unexploded ordnance," Dax explained. "During this discussion, one of the guys brought up this concept of microchipping ordnance. He had recently taken his dog to the vet and had his dog microchipped in case his pet got lost. From that simple example, he came up with the idea of microchipping ordnance for tracking it. Other EOD professionals worked very hard to encourage the tagging of ordnance so that it could be efficiently found and tracked. I never thought that I would actually see the day that the Lost Puppy protocol would be implemented. What happened to make this all come about?"

"Several years ago, a company of marines were easily overrun because, as it was later discovered, their mortar rounds were all defective." The colonel continued, "This lead to a demand for exact failure rates from ordnance manufacturers. Military officials wanted an accurate accounting of duds and demanded overall proofs of efficiency. Since deminers and other EOD personnel are the first to be in contact with unexploded ordnance all of them became a necessary part of the entire process. We are very well equipped with everything we need. We even have detectors built into the skids of our helicopter for landing in areas of suspected contamination."

"So you can fly over and do a few sweeps to know exactly where it would be safe to put the chopper down?" Marcus asked.

"Only the tagged stuff," said the colonel. "For all the older explosives located in every country, you will still have to carry on just as you have in the past."

"Wow! This is so great," said Dax. "This means we can reclaim the land that we had already cleared before this carpet bombing happened. Also we can do it much faster than we ever could. It will also help us find the newer tagged items as we clear additional lands. Can we get one of those new detectors you are using?"

"Right you are!" said the colonel. "We will instruct you and leave you the needed equipment to win your home back. I am just sorry that we don't have a way of assisting you with the rebuilding."

"With some humanitarian aid, we will be able to get back on our feet again," Marcus stated excitedly. "The main thing is that with this new technology we don't have to start from scratch. We will be able to reclaim our land and rebuild much faster than ever. You have no idea what a priceless gift you have brought to us, Colonel Meadows! Thank you!"

"Quite! Well, it must be close to tea time by now. How about sharing a meal together and all of us can take a breather?" the colonel said, directing his men to quit for the day. "Tomorrow at first light, we can get cracking and finish up here. We can combine teams so that your people can learn all about this new technique. Our schedule has us moving on to another location around mid-afternoon."

Dax motioned his team to put up their detectors. "Thank you so much for coming to us. Please bring your crew up to the cave and let us introduce you to our village."

Mama Ha and Gelda were already beginning to cook a celebratory dinner. The aromas coming from the kitchen reached the returning deminers and their new guests. Everyone was looking forward to meeting new people.

Life certainly has unexpected surprises, thought Maria as she looked at Marcus and the other deminers. "No one would have thought that we would be celebrating anything a day after the bombing?" She smiled as that little flutter in her abdomen happened again. Maybe she should see Julikai and have a talk with her. She had a hint as to what may be the cause but would not jump to any conclusions, yet.

Dax had stayed behind for a moment on the newly cleared path. He was overwhelmed with emotions of gratitude at this latest turn of events. Not only had there been not a single casualty from the bombing, but now, there was a renewed hope that this village could rebuild without future casualties. Dax looked around, hoping to spot Trevor, his guardian angel to thank him for watching out for all of them. However, the tall one-legged aboriginal could not be spotted amongst the splintered burned and flattened vegetation. Dax fell to his knees as he realized it was not Trevor who must be thanked for this day. After a few moments of prayerful meditation, Dax got to his feet. He strode up the incline to the entrance of the cave. There was new vitality within him. His walk was youthful and carefree.

Journey Home

One lone person walked across the hot dry plains. The old canvas backpack was well worn by both weather and age. An old cast iron teapot swung from a pack strap as the old man strode on.

Dax had been travelling on foot for almost a week. After a year at the village, his demining assignment was completed. Except for Marcus, who was now the new senior manager in charge, Dax had not said good-bye to anyone. This was his way. He would work until he felt he had contributed all that he could then he would move on. During this journey toward a new but yet unknown destination, he would take time to review all of the experiences and people of the village. He had already started to think about what was to come. He would start again somewhere else. It had always been like this for him and this wandering existence.

Trekking across the continent, he felt that something was different somehow. It felt like he had left a part of himself behind. True, he had given his metal detector to young Lincoln, but he felt that the something missing was not anything material. It made this journey especially unusual.

He was preoccupied with contemplating this new awareness about himself. Dax had always been the world traveler looking forward, never dwelling on the past. Why was this last departure so unique?

The afternoon heat rose up from the dry parched earth. Above him, the radiant sun pierced his frayed boonie hat and plaid shirt.

Dax occasionally took small sips of water from a gallon clay jug that Maria had given to him.

He thought, *Ah, they were a special family: Marcus, Maria, and Jacob.* It was good to know that their new cottage was bigger and better than the old one. "She and Marcus will be having another child soon," Dax said out loud to himself. Their little son Jacob was so excited about this addition to their family. He could not decide whether he wanted a brother or a sister. "Jacob, what a spunky little boy he was. He was a bundle of energy and curiosity." Dax's lips curled up into a big smile as he thought about the little boy and his family. Talking to himself was nothing new to Dax. He was used to chatting away for hours while traveling solo.

His stomach started growling. "Must be getting close to dinner time at the village," Dax said. The old Vietnamese woman would be busy cooking right about now. Mama Ha, what a caring and hard-working old woman she was. She would be there serving some kind of delicious meal to everyone and saying only one word—*ha*—to express her love and concern for all. "Mama Ha," Dax said as he marched on taking another small sip of water. "Ha!"

Another very special person popped into his mind: Julikai. He tried to imagine Julikai and Drayton as husband and wife. "What an odd couple they made," Dax said. She was the compassionate field doctor and he the former mercenary. He had seen this relationship develop during the bombing raid. Since that time, Drayton had accompanied Julikai wherever she went. His protection and care were very evident. As they both became aware of their feelings toward each other, their developing love became as visible as a glow of light. Chuckling as he walked, Dax let out a yell, "What a hoot!" The dust was swirling around his footsteps as he continued on. He had never known Julikai to be so happy. Drayton was a big surprise. "He just had to get over who he had been so that he could move on to being who he needed to be." He contributed a lot to the clearance team and made one heck of a deminer. "What a perfect team Drayton and Julikai made. Together, they became better in helping to mend wounds and discouraged spirits. The village will be better because of them," Dax whispered as he walked.

During the late afternoon, Dax realized that he seemed to be taking more and more rest breaks. "A lifetime of finding and disposing of explosive remnants of war can wear a person out." Again, he was speaking out loud. "Sure hope no one is out here listening to me. They would be thinking that a crazy old man was wandering out here all alone." By dusk, he was quite tired. Up ahead in the hazy approach of darkness, Dax saw Trevor standing there. The Aboriginal was looking down, holding on to little Jacob's hand. Jacob was looking up at Trevor.

"Trevor!" Dax yelled. "Jacob!" As he approached, it became quite clear to him that this was just an apparition. Instead of two familiar faces, the old man was looking at an old rural mailbox with bits of tumbleweed and plastic trash bags hanging down. "My eyes get even worse than usual at dusk or dawn," Dax said, feeling exasperated.

Dax decided to camp right there. No need to push forward anymore for the night. He would use the tumbleweeds and the wooden mailbox post as fuel for his camp fire. Before very much time had passed, he had a pot of tea boiling over the fire. The sparks from the fire seemed to be rising upward reaching toward the stars. In the nearby bushes, he heard and noticed rabbits playing. He set out a small wire snare to try his luck at catching "breakfast." Too tired to do much else, he settled back on his bed roll and soon his mind started to wander—back to the village. It was in the middle of musing he drifted off to sleep.

In his slumber, he saw the deminers all standing around: Marcus, Drayton, Lincoln, Zee, David, and the others…all talking about the day's activities. They were a brave bunch of guys doing a damn good job. He dreamt about his idea for the Lost Puppy and how it now was the protocol of all newly manufactured ordnance. It was being employed throughout the world. Such a simple idea that would track failed ordnance while at the same time save lives through more efficient land clearance. Why did it take ten years to come about? Thank goodness someone had initiated it, and now it had come to fruition.

While dreaming, he could see and hear the sounds of the village. Farmers were going out to the cleared fields, and children could now play anywhere they wanted. People were moving around with a sense of home and security. Even in sleep, Dax was smiling as he roamed around the village in a vision, watching everyone he cared about.

The summer sun was peeking over the horizon as Dax woke up. Feeling older than usual, his trembling muscles got the sore bones to stand up. With only a few stumbling steps, he could see that the rabbit snare was empty. He returned to rummage around in his backpack to see if he could find anything to eat. An old forgotten crumbling biscuit appeared at the bottom. Next to it he found a small white letter-sized envelope. There was a small simple message written on it in Julikai's handwriting. It read simply, "A little taste of home."

Even before he opened it, Dax could smell that it was a bit of the coffee he had brought back from the trading village, Tranquility. Dax smiled at the gift knowing that a lot more people probably knew that he had planned to leave. After making coffee in his teapot, Dax extinguished his morning fire. Within minutes, he had his meager supplies packed and on his back. Adjusting the straps to balance the weight on his shoulders, Dax looked all around. "What a magnificent country this had once been. Before war had come here, this was the land where everyone wanted to live and raise their families," he said.

Dax felt for the white envelope in his shirt pocket. Carefully, he unfolded the written note from Julikai. His eyes focused and concentrated on the word *home*. It seemed as though for the first time in his life, he understood what *home* meant. His heart felt suddenly light as he put the note carefully away. He started walking in the direction of the village, his village, his home. It would be the place that he would live the rest of his life. It was the very best of all of his destinations: back to the people who he most cared for, back to the people he was important to.

Dax's stride was long and energetic. He knew that Trevor was walking beside him. Two voices sang in the stillness of the morning. "Once a jolly swagman camped by a billibong...so he sat as he watched and waited 'til his billy boiled...who'll come a waltzing Matilda with me."

The two marched on, raising dust with each footstep. They past close to a twisted and rusted signpost. At the top of the post was a black and white sign that was full of bullet holes. Still, a person could read, "US Route 66."

Epilogue

The Last War

A field of tall flames seemed to expand in all directions with no end in sight.

"Another day in hell," Ashton, a lesser fallen angel, said.

He was sitting on a lava rock dangling his legs in the fire as if it were a cool lake. Cinderlee, another demon, approached him from behind. She sat down to join him and also dangled her legs into the inferno.

"What's going on, girl?" Ashton asked while spitting into the barely visible coals below. His spit popped and sizzled as it reached its destination.

"Another bus load of Satan worshippers just arrived," Cinderlee answered. "It's always such a surprise to them when we toss them into the fire. They think that there should be a special place for them after all their preaching and sacrifices. When they finally get here, they join everyone else wailing at the bottom of the pit."

Cinderlee and Ashton let out a squealing laugh. They looked at each other as they realized that it had been a few centuries since either of them laughed.

"So the talk around is that we are going on one last campaign," Ashton said in a suddenly serious tone.

"Yes, everyone is unanimous about marching back to heaven," Cinderlee said. "Won't it be strange to see all of our brothers and sisters again after such a long time?"

"Strange indeed!" Ashton answered. "Really, I think this is more frightening than anything else we've ever tried, Cindy."

"True enough. With this confrontation, will we not risk being sent to a place worse than hell?" Cinderlee replied.

After a moment, Ashton replied, "Yes, it is traveling into unknown territory. I cannot remember any of us doing anything brave since we started the first war. I can admit I'm afraid, are you?"

"I sure am. It will be hard to leave all this 'security' behind," Cinderlee said playfully. They both laughed again.

"You know it just occurred to me that even while we are banished from heaven and working every temptation in the book, we are still serving God." Ashton stated. "We take out the trash of humanity, and we all supervise the storage of it here. It's kind of crazy when you think of it."

Cindy grimaced. "Yeah, I see what you mean. But then, isn't fruitlessness, disappointment, frustration, and every other negative emotion part of living in hell?"

"You got that right," Ashton answered. "That is why advancing on heaven now seems to be a really courageous act. If you will excuse me for saying so, it seems very forward thinking."

Cinderlee had a puzzled expression on her face as she said, "Sometimes, I wonder if we should be doing this. Other times, I feel that there is nothing more important, and this is the time to do it."

"Did you hear that we would no longer be causing and creating wars on earth?" Ashton responded. "It seems that casualties of innocent civilians make up about 95 percent of all the losses in armed conflicts. We were actually creating more martyrs for heaven and less souls for hell. No one was winning, least of all us."

"Wow. That makes sense!" Cinderlee said. "So what are we bringing on this march?"

"Nothing," Ashton said. "Lieutenant Sparksin said anything we packed would just slow us down. We are going in with nothing but ourselves."

"My, that really is brave!" Cinderlee responded breathlessly. "Oh, hey, speak of the devil, here comes the boss. I think it's time to go."

Ashton was amazed as he witnessed the gathering together of all the fallen angels into one large assembly. Together, they all moved out as one. There was no chanting or yelling. Quietly, they moved forward each one wondering if it would be wiser to go back now or braver to continue going forward. Individually, each fallen angel had made up their mind to have this encounter in heaven. None of them went back. No one looked back. Each knew what must be done.

Since he was so nervous, Ashton needed to talk as he traveled up the steep incline. Talking with one of his fellow angels he said, "Remember when Hitler came to us? How excited we all were to meet him! Man, what a disappointment he turned out to be. Without his power, he was just another sniveling little coward!"

Suddenly, a hush came over the company of angels. The journey was almost finished for he could see those mighty gates ahead. To make matters more frightening, the gates were already opened. As they approached the entrance, Ashton began swallowing to try to get rid of a lump of hesitation in his throat. He watched as one by one each angel gathered strength as they crossed the threshold. He could see Cinderlee. She knelt just inside the gate. She asked for forgiveness in the part she played during the first war and every bad thing she had done since. She stood up smiling and walked into a warm bright light of acceptance. She looked fresh and without worry as the filth of the past fell away from her form. Each angel in turn experienced the long ago promise of love and forgiveness.

When it was his turn, without hesitation, Ashton walked into the place he had left so many years ago. Falling to his knees, he proclaimed a similar request of reconciliation. He also added a sincere prayer of thanks. He knew he was home. Looking straight in front of him, there stood Trevor.

Standing on the only leg he had, Trevor held out both arms to welcome him back. "Ashton!" Trevor shouted, showing a wide white toothy grin. "Good on ya, mate! That has to be the longest walkabout ever! So you've been a bit lost then? Well, we never quit praying for your return."

"Yes, I've been a bit lost!" Ashton replied. His voice was wavering with emotions he had not felt in a very long time. He moved forward and hugged his brother for the first time in several billion years.

Author's Notes

The purpose of this book is to bring forth, in an entertaining way, some aspects of the world that were previously unknown to the reader. Even the characters are compilations of the many people that I have met during my world travels. Perhaps through meeting these characters the reader may research some of the subjects that are introduced and even find a passion of his or her own. For those who do not know what passion is…it is the very purpose that a person is created. It is the work that energizes you. For some it is sharing music. For others it may be to bring laughter. For me it is removing a bomb's fatal purpose as well as educating people to avoid these things called unexploded ordnance (UXO) which were only created to kill.

This journey of mine started when I began an unexploded ordnance clean-up project on Kaho'olawe Island, Hawaii, in 2001. As a UXO team member I assisted in removing unexploded ordnance, bomb fragments, target material and other contamination placed there after more than fifty years of bombing. It had been used as a target island since the beginning of WW II. When returning from Southeast Asia in my youth our U.S. Navy ship had bombed Kaho'olawe and dumped ordnance in the local Hawaiian waters. I had come full circle by cleaning up the very explosives that I had helped to put there almost thirty years earlier.

It was then out of curiosity that I returned to Southeast Asia to see how those countries survived the long term effects of the Vietnam

War. Without a doubt meeting those young victims of landmines and other residual military explosives changed my life's focus forever. There was one particular eight year old Cambodian girl who brought me to the realization that I could make positive changes in the world. There she was, left out in the jungle heat with no shade, no water, and no food. She was put there to beg from any passing tourist visiting the ancient Ankor Wat temple complex. She had lost both legs to a landmine. It was so tragic, I thought, and so avoidable. It seemed that my redemption, my personal forgiveness, would involve a career of being a part of the solution in preventing this kind of pointless suffering. Not only was I active in removing these dangers from the land world-wide but also felt the need to educate those at risk about UXO avoidance so that there will be fewer casualties in the future.

Working in the field on some very inefficient UXO projects led me to become frustrated with the present situation. I knew that there had to be a better method in clearance then the antiquated methods and equipment we now employ. It was from this experience that the idea to tag ordnance with microchips prior to deployment became a possible option. A secure database and a special detector to identify the unexploded ordnance would need to be developed so that there would be greater efficiency and safety for all. By continuing to communicate with ordnance manufacturers and the Defense Department it is hoped that this possibility may soon become a reality.

For more information on this subject please refer to the following articles:

Imber, Jack "The Need for Collaboration Between Ordnance Manufacturers and UXO Clean-up Personnel" *The Journal of ERW and Mine Action* (Fall 2012) Issue 16.3, pp. 8-10.

Davis, Richard J., Shubert, Keith A., Barnum, Thomas J. and Balaban, Bryan D. "Buried Ordnance Detection: Electromagnetic Modeling of Munition-Mounted Radio Frequency Identification Tags" *IEEE Transactions on Magnetics* (July 2006) Vo. 42 No. 7, pp.1883-1890.

For additional information on mercenaries also known as private military contractors (PMCs) it is suggested to view appropriate documentaries and articles which are presented objectively through VICE News via the Internet.

For further information regarding "Explosive Remnants of War: A World View" a power point presentation as well as other topics which pertain to civilian ordnance safety contact the author at: jack_imber@yahoo.com.

About the Author

Jack Imber has been clearing land of explosive remnants of war during the past thirteen years. As an EOD Level Two and Humanitarian Deminer, Jack is very passionate about encouraging more efficient technologies to improve on antiquated methodologies that are in use now. Proposing ordnance tagging prior to deployment, supporting the development of centralized mine action centers, providing unexploded ordnance awareness and safety presentations to first responders, academia and the public at large are just some of the ongoing humanitarian projects that Jack is currently involved with worldwide. Writing fictional and non-fictional stories is the most recent way in which he is working to initiate more dialog about these most important issues that affect populations long after war's end. His sustaining philosophy is that as long as you are doing what you are supposed to do you will always have what you need to do it. Jack and his wife Elaine live in Savannah Georgia.

CPSIA information can be obtained at www.ICGtesting.com
Printed in the USA
LVOW10s0925230815

451197LV00001B/26/P